The Monk's Path to Joy:

The Art of Living Without Leaving Comfort

Spirituality · Science · Love

By

Subrata Halder

PUGMARK BOOKS
SCIENCE : ART : TRUST : JOY

PUGMARK BOOKS
New Delhi | India

Book Name: **The Monk's Path to Joy**
Author: Subrata Halder

For permissions requests or inquiries regarding this publication,
Please contact:

PUGMARK BOOKS
SCIENCE.ART.TRUST.JOY

Pugmark Books
https://salesskills.co.in/pugmark-book
subrata.halder.pro@gamil.com
+91 9999715748

ISBN: 978-93-5759-596-4

Cover design: by the author
Typesetting: by the author

First Edition: February 2026

Preface

We all have only one life. It is better to accept it than to create unnecessary arguments with it. It is also better to accept that our body, mind, and hormonal secretions will function as they are programmed to. We can delay certain effects through good habits or hasten them by giving excessive priority to momentary enjoyment.

Having said that, today's enjoyment is also a vital part of living life. So, the way out is balance.

It is not only physical balance; we also need to work on our mental setup, because our happiness, pain, and suffering are influenced not only by external factors, but by how we perceive them.

Here, studying good life-related literature helps. This is one of them. In this novel, the main character, a Monk, answers many questions that people have been searching for years. So-called wise men, gurus often do not speak straightforwardly; they mostly beat around the bush and make matters more complicated. The subjects discussed and clarified here can be as complex as the existence of God, or as simple as peace and wealth, yet many people carry negative or half-cooked thoughts about them due to a lack of clarity.

Hold on: by now, you may have started thinking this is just another religious book full of sermons. No. It is an action-packed novel of spirituality, love, and science, meant for every age group. The earlier one reads it, the more one may benefit, while also spending meaningful and enjoyable time reading a novel.

The best gift is gifting a book; we learned this from our ancestors. You may gift this book to young members of your family to encourage them to cultivate the habit of reading good literature.

If one has not studied the great philosophers of the Far East—from Buddha to Confucius to Vivekananda, one will find glimpses of their wisdom here, not as abstract philosophy but woven into engaging storytelling.

Love is a part of the life of every human being, as ultimately every human is an individual identity, and that individuality is highly respected in this novel.

And finally, if the content of the book pleases you, if you feel it has helped you gain knowledge and depth about religion, and if it surprises you with its unique scientific innovation, then please share it with others. If you wish to share your thoughts, my contact details await you on the final page. Readers' feedback is always priceless to a sincere author.

With heartfelt gratitude,
Subrata Halder

For my little granddaughters,
Choco and Candy.

HOLY
BIBLE
BHAGALAD
GITA
QURAN

The Monk's Path to Joy:
The Art of Living Without Leaving Comfort

PART 1

The humdrum boy:

It was not a particularly sad day for the family, even though Rishi, the elder son of the village priest, had failed his secondary school examination. His father and the rest of the household had long since lowered their expectations. No one truly believed that Rishi would excel academically or get a respectable job. Their quiet hope was simpler: that Rishi would eventually join his father's modest business and help manage the household with slightly more ease.

Rishi himself had held on to a sliver of hope. Perhaps, somehow, he might qualify with just enough marks to pass. His overall scores were not terrible, but fate had struck where it hurt most; he had failed three subjects marginally. And ironically, they were the ones he had always detested. History and Chemistry never appealed to him; he had no dreams of becoming a historian or a chemist. As for Geography, he failed not because he lacked interest, but because he believed it wasn't something to be learned from books. To him, the world was meant to be touched and seen, not memorised through maps and definitions.

Yet he had performed well in Biology, English, and Mathematics, his three favourites. Rishi was not a good student by conventional standards, but he was intelligent, curious, and full of energy. Whenever something truly struck his interest, he gave it his all and often excelled. But time was never on his side. Each morning, he would rise early and head to the fields to cut grass for the pair of cows the family owned. Those cows were their livelihood, the real breadwinners of the household. He knew it too. The cows earned for the family. He didn't. And there was little hope he ever would.

In the evenings, after returning from school, Rishi would go door-to-door delivering milk to a few loyal neighbours who trusted his family for their pure, unadulterated product. After that, he often helped his father at the nearby temple. Whatever little free time he found, he spent with his friends playing games, wandering the village paths, or simply idling under the sky. Studies were a distant priority in Rishi's life. There was no ambition driving him, nor any pressure from his family. They were poor, yes, but somehow the household limped along on the meagre but steady earnings from his father's temple duties and tailoring work.

Despite being a priest's son, Rishi had a patchy reputation in the locality. People assumed he would lead an ordinary, uneventful life, perhaps assisting in the temple or continuing the small tailoring shop his father managed, mostly doing odd repairs and mending.

When Rishi returned home after collecting his exam results, his father needed no words. A single glance at Rishi's face was enough to tell him everything.

"No matter, my son. Try again," his father said softly, offering comfort rather than criticism.

However, Rishi felt no desire to try again. He had already made peace with the result, even before he saw the marks.

While his father remained calm, his uncle, the younger brother of his father, who lived nearby, was not so forgiving. This uncle had always played the role of guardian in the family. Whenever there was a financial crunch, he would step in with support. After all, Rishi's father barely earned enough to meet daily expenses. The uncle had long nurtured a hope that Rishi might one day lift the family out of poverty by securing a stable job.

That afternoon, the uncle met Rishi on the road, on his way to the house to hear about the results. Rishi told him the truth. Without a word, his uncle raised his hand and struck him hard. A tight, resounding slap. It echoed not only in Rishi's ears but through every corner of his being. Rishi stood frozen, his head bowed. He had nothing to say. He didn't move. The slap rang on in his skull like a cruel song. It was the first time anyone had hit him and in public, no less.

"You fool!" his uncle shouted. "Do you even understand the consequences of this failure? Your father is poor. You have two younger sisters. Do you think life will wait for you to get serious? You won't be able to find good grooms for your sisters or provide proper treatment for your parents when they fall sick. The man who breaks his back every day just to give you a life of some comfort, he'll die without medicine, without care!"

Then, with a bitter voice, he spat out the final blow. "No issue if you live a bitch-life, but you have no right to drag the rest of your family members down with your laziness and idiocy. Now get out of my sight."

Still, Rishi could not move. He was too humiliated, too stunned to lift his eyes. His uncle stormed off, and Rishi remained a lone figure in the middle of the road. Around him, passers-by had stopped. He didn't need to look up to know they were watching. Judging. Smirking. In that moment, Rishi felt the full weight of his disgrace. No one stood up for him. No one offered a word of sympathy.

That night, sleep eluded him. He lay awake, tormented, uncertain of what path to take. Should he do what his uncle said, study hard and prove himself? Or should he take revenge for the insult? The days rolled by, but Rishi's mind remained unsettled. He wandered the village lanes, hoping to escape his thoughts.

And finally, he made up his mind. Revenge, it seemed, was the only path to peace. However, he fails to decide on the action of revenge.

Town Hall - Fifteen years later:

The grand hall was full, just as expected. The city's mayor, ministers, and a line of dignitaries had begun to arrive for the felicitation ceremony, an event exclusively organised to honour Rishi, the city's most celebrated son. He had spent the best part of his youth in this very town, and now, the town had gathered to honour his journey.

Rishi waited alone in a small, quiet room backstage. The applause from the crowd barely registered in his mind. Instead, he was haunted by a memory from fifteen years ago, a slap that had branded his soul with a pain no time could erase. That moment, so cruel and humiliating, replayed in his mind with an unbearable clarity. His thoughts drifted further into the past. Revenge!

Rishi again went to the past. It was a Sunday, three days after his exam results. Rishi had walked to the riverside, a kilometre from his home, trying to calm his mind and plan his revenge. He sat on a stone-paved ghat by the water, watching the boats ferry people across the river. A cold breeze touched his skin, but it failed to cool the turmoil within him.

Suddenly, chaos erupted. A boat capsized barely a hundred metres from the bank. Rishi didn't take a moment to think. He jumped into the river, forgetting his pain, forgetting everything. He could swim well; he had learned as a child, taught by his father in these very waters. During his teenage years, he often swam here with friends. He had even taken part in a long-distance competition organised by a local club. Though he hadn't won, the experience had built his confidence to battle currents and tides.

When he was pulled from the river, Rishi was only half-conscious. People gathered around him, some out of concern, most out of curiosity. Within an hour, the once-dismissed boy had become a local hero. Rishi had been the first to jump into the water, pulling drowning men and women onto boats. He saved many lives that day, more than a dozen before others arrived to help.

But when he tried to save two men at once, one clutched his throat in terror, nearly choking the breath from him. Rishi refused to let go, knowing the other would drown. Rishi was in big trouble to save himself, but he did not loosen his grip, which was holding two men who were about to die. At that moment, a rescue boat arrived to save all three.

Later that evening, Swami Dayanand ji, head of the renowned Ramakrishna Ashram, arrived at Rishi's modest home. He bowed before Rishi's father, a gesture that stunned the family. Most people folded their hands before the monk in reverence. But Swami ji, deeply moved, pleaded with Rishi's father to allow him to take the boy to his Ashram and fund his entire education. Rishi's father hesitated. He depended on Rishi's help for daily survival. Rishi himself was torn. How could he leave his struggling family behind for his own future?

But then, his uncle, whose voice always decided family matters, spoke firmly. "Swami ji, do not embarrass us by requesting. We take your words as divine will. Let Rishi go and see a new life. I will take care of my elder brother's family. Please bless him."

Rishi's mother alone had no words. She was silently standing holding the kitchen door, her eyes swollen but dry. She was the only one who didn't resist, for she could already see the path unfolding before her son, a path painted with the hues of destiny. She cried the most, but her tears were not of despair. They were a mixture of hope and heartbreak. Because she is a mother.

Rishi flourished at the Ashram. The teachers there were more than educators; they were devotees who taught not for money but out of spiritual commitment. The curriculum was rigorous, designed to shape strong minds and stronger hearts. Yet, what pushed Rishi wasn't just the system. It was the sting of a memory, the sound of that slap and the bitter voice that called his life worthless. Those scars made him run faster, study harder, and dream bolder.

A knock at the door brought Rishi back to the present. A person stepped into the backstage greenroom, checking if everything was comfortable.

Rishi nodded gently. He had demanded to be left alone before the event. He needed the silence to focus his mind. The speech he was about to deliver wasn't like the hundreds he had given around the world.

This one would be different. This one could shatter illusions, challenge beliefs, and redefine the very foundation on which people had built their faith in him. This would be the blast.

Rishi again started recalling his journey for a little over a decade. He had not only passed secondary examination with distinction, but he soared higher with every academic milestone. Eventually, he earned a Ph.D. in Biology and joined Purdue University as a professor and researcher. Yet, that was not what brought him to this stage. What made him a global icon was a philosophy he had shaped, not invented, but resurrected. He had introduced the world to a spiritual ideology that was ancient at heart yet modern in expression. The wisdom of past sages was timeless, but Rishi knew that the way it had been presented was no longer relevant for today's world.

He became known globally as Swami Rishavanand, a monk of knowledge, science, and soul. His voice was like the resonant vibration of a violoncello. It didn't just fill rooms; it filled hearts. His lectures were packed beyond capacity, and even critics could not dismiss his impact.

Rishi often recalled when the seed of this transformation was planted within his mind and body. Each morning at the Ashram, before sunrise, he would open his window. In the dim glow of dawn, he would gaze at the statue of Swami Vivekananda standing tall in the garden. That statue wasn't just a sculpture; it was a godlike presence. Its eyes, its strength, and its wisdom awakened something in Rishi.

He read everything he could about the great monk. He learned how Vivekananda was more than a religious figure; he was a national visionary. Titans like Jamshedji Tata had reshaped India under his influence. Institutions like the Indian Institute of Science were inspired by his thoughts. Swami Vivekananda spoke more of people, life, and the self-reliance of individuals and the country than of God and religion, though he was one of the most religious persons and philosophers the world had ever seen. He offered a profound description of Hinduism, transcending narrow, localised interpretations that often weaken the faith through internal conflicts and competing claims of superiority. He also highlighted how religion can be a blessing for the common man, yet a source of harm when misused or distorted by ignorance. Netaji Subhas Chandra Bose described him as a *full-blooded masculine personality* and a fighter to the core, both in religion and in the concept of self-reliance.

After completing his Ph.D., Rishi wanted to join the Ramakrishna Ashram School as a teacher to build the careers of hundreds of students the way Swami Dayanand ji had built his. However, understanding his high potential to do bigger work for mankind, the Ashram committee suggested he take on whatever greater opportunity might come his way. They wanted Rishi to change the lives of millions and billions, not just a few hundred in a school. Rishi accepted and became Swami Rishavanand.

Proactivity-Panorama:

He began spreading his philosophy, blending biology with spirituality. A new concept, crafted from his acquired knowledge through a deep study of the vision of great philosophers across thousands of years. He restructured the thoughts to make them contemporary, as the world had undergone phenomenal changes in the last century. He realised that thoughts over a hundred years old could no longer be presented or accepted, as they had become impractical for the common man today.

The fundamental ideas of great philosophers like *Adi Shankaracharya, Confucius, Buddha, Yoganand Ji Maharaj, Hegel, Karl Marx, Sri Aurobindo, Achariya Rajnish, Rabindranath Thakur, J. Krishnamurti, Ramakrishna Paramhansa, and Swami Vivekananda* were pure and never changed, but their implications varied vastly in this ever-changing, dynamic world. So, Rishi began blending these ideas with modern life, forming an unassailable religious thought for the twenty-first century. The fusion of his superior knowledge of biology and philosophy started showing people across the globe a unique path of life.

After leaving Purdue University, he began delivering lectures at universities and social organisations, which became very popular in a short time. His first talk at the Cambridge University Hall left the audience spellbound and received wide coverage in electronic and print media. The basic concept was not very unique, but contemporary and the presentation was deeply moving, showing how we can be proactive in life to remain happy and healthy.

He started hailing the tiniest visible creature of God to give a jolt to the so-called educated society regarding their lifestyle and intellect.

He asked, "Do you know which one is the most intelligent, powerful, disciplined, and creative living creature on earth?

I am sure the names that spontaneously come to our mind are humans, blue whales, and dolphins because of their unique characteristics, but none of them score high in all of these cumulatively.

Some of you may think of jackals, recalling our childhood fantasy, as we all read a lot of stories about the jackal's intellect. However, it's not jackals; it is one of the smallest creatures visible to the naked eye.

No, it is not a mosquito, though the survival strategy of a mosquito is beyond scientists' knowledge. The dinosaurs even vanished, whatever might have been the reason, be it comet bombardment, temperature rise, etc., but mosquitoes, cockroaches, etc., survived.

Even, despite today's poisonous chemicals and machines developed for the mass killing of these creatures, they have developed their own survival tricks.

However, the words intelligent, disciplined, and powerful together do not apply to them.

Yes, I am talking about ants.

They have a body mass of a milligram and a brain weight in micrograms, which is a billion times less than ours.

However, they are the only God's creation on earth that can lift five hundred times their body weight. It is equivalent to a man lifting a truck or a small house over his head. Is it possible, or can we even imagine it? And not only lifting, but walking millions of times their body length, which is equivalent to us walking from Delhi to Mumbai with a truck on our head. What is the source of that energy, power, and courage?

Ants are the most disciplined and intelligent creatures on earth. Everyone is an ideal team player. Without any engineering knowledge, they create anthills, which is a much more complicated task than making a hundred-storey tower underground by a group of humans.

And the marvel of their engineering is that even though the area gets flooded with water, neither does the water go inside, nor do they have any survival issues.

The second point, survival fitness, is the focus of my discussion here. How they detect forthcoming rain with such a tiny brain is still a miracle. They start accumulating food and take safe shelter before the rain arrives. They break seeds into halves or one-fourths so the seeds cannot grow further in the presence of water, and remain intact as a food for years. Who gave them this knowledge? Moreover, who gave them the knowledge that which seed even grows as half and needs to be broken into four pieces?

They do the same before winter, and it is beyond imagination how they can predict winter in advance and understand that there may be survival challenges during it, especially when the average lifespan of an ant is less than a year, so they have never actually experienced winter.

How does that proactivity come? What is the unique fragment in their gene that gives them such superb foresight and makes them so proactive? Proactivity was the subject of his research as well as his talk, which he named 'Proactivity-Panorama'.

We human beings should learn from the ant how we can apply a proactive approach to lead a happy and healthy life. How much procrastination damages us by getting too involved in other things, neglecting our body and social behavioural aspects.

Happiness can be achieved at any stage of life, but health damage is not reversible. After a heart attack, the heart and body cannot be reconfigured as they were before. Undo does not work in life. However, it is easy to prevent a heart attack if we learn from an ant.

So, one should not wait until middle or old age to converge his/her focus on health; it should be done at a very young age, even while maintaining a good social life. Why wait until fifty to get a kick from high blood pressure or sugar? Start the right diet and exercise at thirty, the true crossover age for physical changes. Shape your mind as well as your physical attributes."

Rishi started blending this with his deep knowledge of biology and physiology as a scientist, along with his philosophical excellence.

Rishi often quoted Swami Vivekananda, who once said, *"It is better to play football than pray in a temple if you want to reach God."* Rishi said, "to pray, you must be strong enough to stand firm. By being strong enough to help others in their journey, you bring yourself closer to God. However, the other reason for Swami Vivekananda's suggestion, he conveyed indirectly in British-ruled India to create able young and energetic fighters for the independence movement."

Rishi reminded the world: "You don't need to become a monk to be spiritual. You need to be honest, disciplined, and proactive.

You can live with your family, work hard, and still nurture your soul."

He loved the metaphor of Sri Ramakrishna: *"Live like a bird. She looks ahead, yet her heart and mind are on the eggs beneath her, which she is incubating to give birth to another soul."* Rishi aligns that with our living saying, Live for the world, give back to Earth, but keep your inner eye on your purpose. The world didn't need more monks. It needed honest, healthy, spiritually aware citizens.

Rishi's movement transcended religion, caste, and even country. He reminded people of what Confucius once said: *"Three things cannot be long hidden, the Sun, the Moon, and the Truth."*

And to find that truth, you must first be honest with yourself and with those around you. Self-honesty and honesty in others in daily life help build happiness from within. Happiness is not a destination or a goal, but something within a person that needs to be kept alive.

All this was said over two thousand years ago by Buddha, yet the fact that we didn't popularise or practice it remains one of the greatest challenges in today's world. People widely accepted Rishi's idea and guidance that instead of inviting trouble through negligence and then scrambling to fix it, one should be proactively sincere to prevent it in the first place.

We all acknowledge that the West is highly advanced in scientific innovation. However, blindly following everything from the West has become a significant concern for the world. Western civilisation is around five hundred years old, whereas Eastern civilisation spans over five thousand years. Long ago, our visionary ancestors in India and China discovered profound truths about life and the universe. They captured these insights in texts like the Geeta, the Upanishads, which are a part of the Veda, and other sacred scriptures. Often mislabelled as merely religious books, these works are in fact profound guides for inner transformation, healthy living, and harmonious coexistence in society, even being a common man.

In Rishi's view, why should one feel the need to follow the life of a yogi or monk? And how practical is that path, really? Not everyone is fortunate enough to have lifelong financial security that allows them to care for their family and then renounce the world in pursuit of a monk's life. And, in truth, it isn't necessary either. People appreciated Rishi's honesty, perhaps the first time a monk had openly declared that becoming a monk is not the goal. One can live in the world and yet be as disciplined and proactive as a monk, especially when it comes to one's health and responsibilities.

Abandoning family and wealth is not wise advice. One can live a beautiful and meaningful life while remaining in society, as Sri Ramakrishna once explained through a beautiful example in his inimitable style. For ordinary people, family is the first priority, as Sri Ramakrishna said over a century ago. Despite being one of the most revered priests, he himself was also a married family man.

Even for the sake of argument, if we agree that living like a Yogi is the ultimate goal and is theoretically possible that everyone turns into a Yogi, is there enough space in ashrams to accommodate one billion people in our country or ten billion across the world? Then how can it be the goal?

If no greater goal, then the advice to lead a monk's life may sound noble in books or discussions, but in reality, it is simply impractical. No goal applies to all, but just a thought that few can only adopt.

Who would grow food, offer services, or build infrastructure if everyone were to become a monk? If we were to take that idea seriously and act on it, society itself would collapse. No monk said this earlier. All said the ultimate goal is spirituality to achieve ultimate happiness, and they glorified a monk's life over the common man's, a dishonest suggestion, knowing it is impractical advice to people. As such, Rishi started becoming popular around the world, and his thoughts were spreading like an inferno across the countries.

People began to understand Rishi's views on life, society, and religion, not because they were entirely new, but because of the clear and relatable way he presented them to millions across his programs. That clarity made a deep impact.

After his successful lecture at Cambridge University Hall, he gained worldwide recognition. Invitations poured in from countries across the globe, and he continued spreading his thoughts and insights. In his view, what he spoke of was not a new religion; it was an essence extracted from different religions, refined for contemporary times. His idea could serve as a true unifying faith, one that transcends specific beliefs and boundaries.

However, his view on the existence of God sparked considerable controversy. Even so, many prominent thinkers agreed that this was perhaps the clearest and most realistic view of God ever presented.

Existence of God:

So, what was Rishi's view? Does God really exist? Unlike other celebrities who avoid the question with hazy, safe explanations, he did not bypass it.

He said, "Yes." Yet while saying "Yes," he also cautioned people with a "No." He explained why the answer is "Yes," and also why, even if it is yes, one must sometimes say no. This is the most critical point that not only ordinary people but also so-called religious gurus and so-called atheists fail to grasp. Missing this point creates confusion and builds a never-ending, unsolvable equation.

He says God exists not in the form that billions believe in. That perception exists mostly to anchor people within a particular religion, which is good. He explained the benefits of it to concentrate the mind towards the Almighty and hail good thoughts in life and society.

God is, in truth, a power, an energy, beyond the capacity of the human mind to fully comprehend. God truly exists. Whatever that power is, it is surely not represented by the various images, holy books or abstract concepts we worship or talk about. As this power lies beyond our understanding, we can consider it like the unknown variable in mathematics, what we call X. Even if there are multiple such powers, there would be no conflict between them. After all, if supreme beings were to clash, the world would not have survived. Rather, we must believe that this unified power, this God, is here to help us all.

So then, why do we complicate things by turning X into Xa, Xb, Xc, many unknown variables, each with its own label and formula, leading to tangled equations with no meaningful solution?

Here, Rishi quoted Sri Ramakrishna and narrated a simple yet profound story.

In a pond, there were four ghats (stairways) on four corners to access the water.

At one corner, a Hindu came to collect 'Jaal'.

At another, a Muslim came to take 'Pani'.

In the third corner, a Christian arrived to draw Water.

In the fourth, an environmentalist took a sample in a test tube, labelling it H_2O.

Whatever names we use- Jaal, Pani, Water, H_2O, the substance is the same.

Up to this point, everything is fine. But the trouble begins when each group insists that their term, their belief, their version is the only true one. That is ridiculous. The water is the same; neither the Hindu, nor the Muslim, Christian, nor the scientist can say their water is better or purer. Who are we to demand it, and if we demanded that, it would be called ignorance and not knowledge.

Belief systems often blind the mind. And when a person becomes blind, they must rely on others to lead them. It becomes even more dangerous when the blind start fighting one another, humiliating humanity in the process, and real disrespect for God takes birth there.

Do we really believe that God, who is the super-creator and supreme controller of the universe, needs our protection? And do we really believe that the messages written in religious texts were directly dictated by God? If you truly believe that, then perhaps nothing could be more naive. Having said that, these messages are good for leading a life with peace and success. However, it is also true that not all these are positive, and many such negative messages should be avoided instead of keeping blind faith and believing whatever is written in these books is holy.

Is it not more likely that these messages were written by people whose livelihood depended on religion, some people who crafted belief systems and then exploited a large number of gullible people?

These divisions not only dilute the truth but also weaken human unity, empowering those who wish to keep humanity divided and vulnerable. That's why a subtle fear lingers everywhere. Most religious messages are saturated with war, suffering, and threats of eternal punishment. Can such messages truly be from a loving and compassionate God?

Initially, people were reluctant to accept Rishi's views. They clashed with deeply ingrained beliefs passed down for generations. However, Rishi's unique style of analysis and storytelling slowly began to spark thought. And according to Rishi, that was his real goal, not to convert, but to get people thinking. The hardest challenge is breaking through stubbornness and mental boundaries. The most difficult task is convincing a person to apply their mind and think.

The presence of God, or a supreme power, is real. But our minds are limited; we can only think about what we already know. That's why some people easily conclude there is no God. They base their judgment on temples, mosques, churches, or a virtual heaven, because those are the only reference points they have. They feel they are intelligent, but they are also the victim of the pride feeling that they know all, they know science. Science itself says about the limitation. Rishi explained that with several good examples.

Rishi explained in an easy-to-understand manner that this is the reason he was utterly popular across the cross-section of society. Think of a place where humans do not live, and monkeys are the most intelligent beings. Try convincing them that a metal aircraft can fly in the sky. The smartest monkey would likely throw a stone to a distance and say, "If even this small stone falls," he would argue, "how can tons of metal remain in the air?".

Did you notice that the monkey used his scientific mind and behaved like a scientist? He disagreed with the reasoning. The problem is that the scientific mind never realises that they are basically wrong when they think they are supreme in this matter. The view of the intelligent monkey is scientifically correct based on his scientific knowledge. Since they lack knowledge of aerodynamics and have never seen an aeroplane, they'd conclude that such an idea is absurd. The issue is the same at a higher orbit for the human being when we refer to science, sometimes, anticipating that science is the ultimate. Science also has very poor reference points, as ever evolving for centuries, and no one knows how much we really know as on date.

Science is supreme in many areas, but not everywhere. Taking it as the final word on all matters is also a kind of blindness. Unfortunately, even many scientists fail to understand this. Some of them live in a fool's paradise, thinking their knowledge is ultimate, and they discard many things, stamping those as unscientific.

Our minds are programmed to perceive only up to a certain limit. Can an ordinary person truly imagine a fourth dimension? No!

Imagine a world where beings can only perceive two dimensions. To them, a chapati (flatbread) and a ball would appear the same.

You cannot convince them that a ball is a three-dimensional object because their perception ends at two dimensions.

Now imagine, for the sake of argument, that there might be a fifth dimension, one that could reveal the existence of God. But we cannot think in those terms. Our brains are not wired for that. And this fifth dimension wouldn't be a physical dimension like the second or third. Think about Einstein's idea of the fourth dimension: it has nothing to do with physical space, but with time. Who knows, there can be fifth, sixth and several dimensions that people can not even think. So, the mystery of proving the existence of god will remain an unsolved equation.

In the same way, we live with a very limited thinking capacity, shaped entirely by our own experiences. And with such limitations, some people conclude that God does not exist. Isn't that a bit foolish?

And yet, sometimes we feel the presence of that higher power. Not everything in life can be explained by religious doctrine or science, because our thought process is simply too limited. Like, a two-dimensional world can not think of a ball, but they sometimes can realise a ball can roll, but a chapati (flatbread) can not be thought both look the same. They fail to find any scientific reason for that, as their knowledge is limited to two dimensions, just as our knowledge is limited to a few dimensions only. Our science and scientific mind stop thinking beyond this point, where philosophy starts its journey.

Up to this point, there's no conflict. The conflict begins when so-called intellectuals believe that humans have reached their intellectual peak and therefore dismiss the possibility of God entirely.

It's also true that we may never fully comprehend God. The human mind is not designed for that. But still, worship and meditation give us strength, confidence, and peace. Faith in God brings blessings.

There are many misfortunes in life that we cannot explain. We cannot see what will happen tomorrow, and so the mind naturally becomes fearful. Yet, most of the things we fear never actually come true. This is where belief in God helps. It gives us the confidence to believe that whatever happens will ultimately serve the greater good for ourselves, our families, and society. As long as it is not harming others, and we find solace in practising religion, it is good in all respects.

Here, the existence of idols, or mandirs, masjids, churches, gurudwaras, stupas, and dozens of other religious establishments is meant to help people concentrate their minds on humanity and worship. Over time, some followers turned into blind supporters and began misusing these institutions. This is a reality that has existed since the earliest naive stages of the God concept thousands of years ago, not just in the twenty-first century. Religion itself should not be blamed for this; rather, people need to be more educated.

In a nutshell, proper education means that whatever we do in the name of religion should not harm even a single individual. The mantra must be "We treat each other with equal respect". We do not need to follow what is written in religious books word for word, but we should understand what is within them truly serves mankind. Most rituals were created by people who earned their livelihood through religious practices, and whether we choose to follow them or not determines our religiousness. Even if we do not follow any of those rituals, we can still be religious. Therefore, going to a religious establishment and praying is perfectly fine, as long as it is done with wisdom.

After explaining God from a completely different perspective, often using profound scientific reasoning, Rishavanand ji would frequently conclude such discussions with real-life stories. One such tale goes like this:

An atheist professor entered the classroom and immediately threw a question at his students: "Is every human being in this world a child of God?"

One student, with confidence, replied, "Yes, sir."

"Really?" The professor gave a slight smile after hearing the student's answer. "Are you sure? Have you thought this through?"

When the student again confidently replied in the affirmative, the professor continued, "If every human being is his child, then evil as well. According to your logic, evil exists; that would mean God Himself is evil because He created all the qualities of both good and bad in us."

Hearing such words, the whole class fell silent. No one dared to speak. Seeing the students' silence, the professor felt rather pleased with himself.

After a while, another student stood up.

In a cheerful tone, the professor asked, "You want to say something?"

The student smiled and asked, "Sir, may I ask you a question?"

"Of course," said the professor.

The student asked, "Sir, does cold actually exist?"

The professor's expression turned irritated. "What kind of silly question is that? Why wouldn't cold exist? Of course, cold exists. Haven't you ever felt cold?"

The student replied with a smile, "Actually, sir, cold does not exist. What we refer to as 'cold' is, in terms of physics, merely the absence of heat. The word 'cold' is just used to describe the lack or reduction of heat."

After a short pause, the student asked again, "Sir, does darkness exist?"

The professor replied, "Why wouldn't it? Of course, darkness exists."

With a smile, the student responded, "Your understanding is incorrect, sir.

Darkness does not exist. We can research light, measure its wavelength, and calculate its speed. But because darkness does not exist in itself, we can't study it in any way. A tiny ray of light is enough to eliminate darkness, but darkness can never consume light because darkness is not a thing; it's merely the absence of light."

The student asked one final question: "Now, sir, would you say that evil exists?"

The professor, now a bit agitated, replied, "Of course it does! Every day, people are murdered, injustices occur, aren't those evil?"

The student responded with strong conviction,

"*No, sir. Evil does not truly exist. It is merely the absence of good, just like cold is the absence of heat, and darkness the absence of light. Evil arises when there is an absence of empathy, a void of love for God in a person's heart. What we perceive as evil or wrongdoing is simply that emptiness. When God is present in the heart, it becomes filled with compassion, kindness, and inner joy. A person blessed by God cannot engage in sin."*

That student was none other than Narendranath Dutta, who is known across the world today as Swami Vivekananda. It beautifully reflects that although Swami Vivekananda became immensely popular after his historic speech at the Chicago Parliament of Religions, he was, in fact, born with an extraordinary intellect and wisdom.

People gradually began to appreciate and embrace Rishi's unique way of explaining the concept of uniformity.

Rishavanand Ji's mind was clear: yes, the power we call God exists. A pure mind can feel it, but it will never be able to prove it. Our brain is not wired for that. A good belief acts as a positive force in our lives, unless it becomes excessive or forceful.

Peace:

Most people, we observed, tried to bring peace into their lives by embracing religion, yoga, or meditation. But they ignored the essential foundations: honesty, ethics, and empathy. One cannot attain peace in isolation. Peace is not a private retreat but a collective cleansing of the mind. Just as cleaning your own home is futile if the surroundings remain filthy, inner peace is meaningless if the world around you suffers from turmoil.

To illustrate this, Rishi often turned to a beautiful parable said by Sri Ramakrishna. One day, three friends came upon a tall wall. Curious about what lay on the other side, they decided to investigate. With great effort, one of them managed to climb up. As soon as he peeked over, his face broke into a wide grin, and with uncontainable joy, he jumped to the other side without a word. The remaining two were stunned. What could he have seen that made him react like that?

The second friend, now even more curious, climbed the wall. His face lit up with the same delight, and he too leapt over, disappearing beyond the wall.

Now only the third remained. He struggled up the wall and finally saw it a world filled with joy, festivity, and bliss. He was about to jump like the others, but then a thought struck him: "What about the people in our village? They are still suffering, their lives burdened with endless struggles. Who will bring them this good news if I leave, too? So, let me go back and we shall go there together."

So, instead of jumping, he turned back to guide the others toward that world of joy. The story was metaphorical, of course, but it conveyed more than a thousand sermons. It's a bit like the ant society that Rishi used to talk about. When an ant finds food somewhere, it never starts eating; it immediately turns back to inform the others, so they can gather more and benefit together more. They seem to understand that life isn't meant to be enjoyed alone, especially when you're such a tiny creature.

As Swami Vivekananda proclaimed, *"Arise, awake, and stop not till the goal is reached."* This goal is not merely about personal success; it is inclusive, meant for the upliftment of all. True progress lies in raising ourselves while raising others, in walking the path not alone but with compassion, awareness, and a sense of duty toward humanity.

But when we call an ant tiny, so they need to support each other, we often forget that we, too, are tiny creatures, if you consider the scale of the world or the vastness of the universe. So, look beyond your own narrow boundaries because sustainable peace is not an individualistic matter.

Rishi emphasised that one must truly believe that God sees everything. If that is the case, then why not commit only to good deeds? A wrongdoing knowingly, for example, paying or accepting a bribe or achieving something by depriving a deserving candidate, cannot be undone by simply doing something good later, because God is not blind, nor does God get satisfied with expensive rituals, fasting, or self-inflicted punishment, if the person is not honest by heart. You may ask forgiveness for small mistakes, but if wrongdoing becomes a pattern, and excuses pile up like "Everyone does it," or "I'm only doing it for my family," then you're only fooling yourself, not God. Confucius said, *"It is better to light a candle than to curse the darkness."* Though the same phrase appears with other names also but the message is very clear.

Stop doing wrong. Stop participating in the rat race that fuels greed, corruption, and dishonesty. Do not intentionally harm anyone. For unintentional mistakes, seek forgiveness, whether from God or from those you have hurt. Say sorry, but make sure it doesn't become a convenient habit to shield your repeated failures. Strive to help others, and if you're not in a position to help, at the very least, don't harm.

This philosophy was beautifully echoed in the timeless words of Confucius: *"Do not do to others what you cannot bear yourself."*

Rishavanand ji often referred to the teachings of Karma Yoga as narrated by Swami Vivekananda. He explained that there are generally two kinds of people in the world: those filled with positive thoughts and those consumed by negative thoughts. Interestingly, both types of individuals have a powerful influence on the people around them.

Those with positive minds are clear, compassionate, and uplifting. Their very presence encourages others to walk the path of progress. In contrast, those governed by negativity tend to spread anger, jealousy, and other destructive emotions, not only harming themselves but also affecting everyone they come into contact with. Mixing with positive individuals creates a subtle aura around us, which in turn attracts more positivity. Thoughts are not just mental phenomena; they radiate waves and silently influence others.

Swami Vivekananda emphasised that we must take our work as worship, without expecting personal gain or recognition. Sri Ramakrishna too advised: "Do not work for the result, but work sincerely, the result is bound to come." Even the smallest sincere efforts, when repeated consistently, can eventually lead to great achievements.

This strength of mind and clarity of purpose do not come overnight. Just as one cannot leap to the top of a high-rise building, not even to the first floor, but needs to take several small steps and rise steadily. Following the same process, growth must happen step by step. There is no shortcut, no lift. One must climb patiently, one step at a time. To do this, we need to spend time with ourselves, cultivate positivity, and strive each day, even if in a small way. A minuscule effort each day, when multiplied over a year, becomes 365 steps closer to the goal, a journey toward personal and spiritual evolution.

Kaizen, developed in post-World War II Japan, literally means "continuous improvement." It was popularised by Toyota and other Japanese firms as a structured approach to enhance productivity, quality, and workplace culture.

Yet, when we speak of Kaizen, we often forget that the very seed of this philosophy was articulated much earlier in Karma Yoga as narrated by Swami Vivekananda. Let us look a little deeper into the striking similarities between the two.

- *Continuous refinement of character* in Karma Yoga mirrors *continuous improvement* in Kaizen.
- Karma Yoga emphasises *focus on duty, not merely results,* while Kaizen *stresses focus on the process, not merely outcomes.*
- *Selflessness and service* in Karma Yoga find their reflection in *teamwork and humility* within Kaizen.

- And most importantly, the idea of *daily work as spiritual practice and small, steady progress,* which Swamiji beautifully explained in Karma Yoga, resonates with Kaizen's *emphasis on discipline and incremental steps.*

The irony is that many of us remain unaware of or even undervalue the profound life lessons gifted by our own spiritual masters, while readily celebrating similar concepts imported from abroad. If we look deeply, we may discover that what modern management frames as "lessons" already existed in our ancient wisdom, comprehensive life principles woven into a culture that spans over five thousand years.

Rishavanand Ji has re-emphasised, time and again, the importance of surfacing the great lessons of ancient times, which can be meaningfully adapted to modern life.

Mistakes are inevitable, but they are not to be feared. In fact, mistakes can sometimes become blessings. Our minds are full of both good and bad impulses. What matters is our awareness and the ability to learn, not repeating the same errors again and again. Ultimately, it is we who choose which path to follow.

Swami Vivekananda reminded us that God does not live outside; He lives within. If we fill our minds and bodies with negative thoughts and wrong actions, we are offering the Divine a polluted space to dwell in. In that condition, visiting temples, mosques, or churches may not bear fruit. But if we strive to keep our mind and body pure, if we treat each action as a form of devotion, then our prayers, our work, and our lives will bring us closer to the Divine.

These weren't new ideas. But the way Rishavanand ji explained them, framed in everyday situations, in modern language, and delivered across continents, was what made his message profound. His lectures revealed not only his wisdom but also his understanding of geography, culture, and human psychology. His insights seeped into people's hearts, guiding them one step closer to true spirituality.

And what was true spirituality to him? It is like the bird living life naturally, gracefully, with an inner eye always watching the Divine. Let God feel proud of your goodness, not suffer from your sins. If you truly love Him, don't torture Him by doing wrong repeatedly.

Rishavanand ji would often quote age-old truths that were surprisingly unknown to many. The beauty lay in his simplicity; he made them accessible to everyone, regardless of education or status.

You didn't need to travel across the world, climb snow-capped peaks, or dive into deep oceans to experience divine beauty. You could find it on the dewdrop resting gently on the tip of a grass near your cottage, if only you have the eyes and heart to see it. This, Rishavanand ji reminded his audience, was what the great poet-philosopher Kabiguru Rabindranath Thakur had taught us over a century ago, in poetic form that still sang with relevance.

Likewise, one need not renounce every joy in life to draw close to the Divine. Remember, God created you with both light and shadow, and you have every right to experience life fully, so long as your actions do not harm other human beings and nature, as well as your own body and mind. What truly matters is your heart, your thoughts, and your intentions. Without these, even the ascetic path may feel hollow. But with them, even the simplest life can radiate with divine presence.

Every word of Rishavanand ji flowed like a cool, shimmering dewdrop on a fresh morning, calming, cleansing, and revitalising.

Rishavanand ji's favourite story he used to speak at the end, made many people cry and helped to feel how happy we are just because we live in a civilised world. It helps to ignore what we do not have, as we have plenty of reasons to live safely and live in peace.

Rishavanand ji explains that life often confronts us with unhappiness, disappointment, and discouragement when reality refuses to align with our wishes. But sometimes, a certain story can help you rise above those sorrows. You begin to see that, despite life's challenges, you have been spared the worst cruelties this world can offer and that you are, in truth, living a blessed life.

This is related to Raja Rammohan Roy, India's First Modern Man and reformer. It is not a story but the reality of those days.

"If people oppose, whom should I fight for? For whom should I risk my life? Damn it, what's the point in fighting anymore?" Raja Rammohan Roy paced restlessly across his drawing room, muttering to himself.

At that moment, the doorman entered and announced, "An old Brahmin wants to meet you."

"I don't have time now," Rammohan replied curtly.

"I told him so," the doorman continued, "but he refuses to leave."

With a sigh, Rammohan said, "Alright, send him in."

An elderly Brahmin entered. He wore a short dhoti, a nameable draped across his chest, and a tiki on his head. The sight irritated Rammohan Roy, those symbols of orthodoxy he had fought against. His tone turned sharp.

"What do you want?"

The Brahmin's voice trembled as he began.

"I am Mahadev Bhattacharya from Nadia..."

He paused for a moment, struggling to steady himself. Then the words poured out.

"It was a hot, humid day in the month of Baisakh. I had just returned from the toll. My little daughter Aparna leapt into my lap, handed me a glass of water, brought me a towel, wiped my sweat, and fanned me with a handmade pankha. She was only a child, but to her, I was her entire world. 'Baba' on her sweet voice always pleases my heart. How fortunate I am to have such a beautiful daughter.

As we played together, her mother, Mandira, called from the small kitchen on the verandah:

'Aparna is already seven years old. How much longer will you keep her at home? The neighbours tell me every day, find her a husband, a kulin Brahmin, without delay.'

I replied, 'Where will I find such a groom? No one will marry for less than a thousand rupees.'

Mandira whispered back, 'Not everyone is so lucky. But caste and religion must be preserved. Yesterday, a noble Brahmin came to the neighbouring village. He's old around seventy but from a great lineage. He has been rescuing Brahmin brides for just fifty rupees. Give Aparna to him.'

Aparna, with no idea what marriage meant, asked me, 'Baba, what is Mother saying?'

I shouted at Mandira, 'No! This will not happen!' But I felt the weight of the neighbours' words, the unrelenting pressure of samaj, society. And after battling with myself for days, I gave in.

Aparna looked like a goddess in her red choli, bangles, jewellery, alta, and sindoor. She didn't understand the rituals or the old man beside her. The next day, the so-called husband left for another village to rescue another bride, promising to return in a year.

Life went on. Aparna was always by my side, learning household chores from her mother, except cooking. She had once burned her finger slightly, leaving a blister, and from then on was terrified of fire. I told Mandira never to teach her cooking. Aparna was delighted, hugging me tightly. 'Yes, Baba, I'm afraid of fire. Promise me you'll never let Mamma take me near it. I'll learn everything else.' I promised her.

When Ashwin came and Durga Puja approached, I bought her a red saree and alta from the market. She beamed with joy.

'Baba, when will I wear these? Will I look like a queen?' My heart overflowed with happiness.

But the next day… the very next day… a messenger came from her in-laws' house. Narayan Banerjee, my daughter's husband for a few hours, had died. The elders decreed she must commit Sati.

I wanted to tear the letter to shreds, but the messenger had already informed the village elders.

Rammohan Roy leaned forward, his voice tense. "What happened then?"

The villagers threatened to take her by force if I refused. So, I dressed her in the red choli, saree, jewellery, alta, and sindoor. She looked breathtaking. The dhak drums played, the village celebrated, and people smeared her forehead with vermilion, her feet with alta. They brought her favourite curd and sweets. She was thrilled, feeding me with her little hands, still unaware of what the celebration meant.

Then came the order: the pyre was ready at the riverbank. I carried her in my arms. I didn't cry. I didn't want her to suspect anything. At the pyre, all the rituals were performed. She looked at the flames in surprise.

When the fire was lit and the pyre roared, she whispered, 'Baba, let's go home. You know I'm scared of fire.'

I told her, 'Don't worry, Maa, I'm here,' holding her tightly as my hands trembled. She wrapped her soft arms around my neck. And then... I loosened her grip and threw her into the fire.

From within the flames came the piercing scream that will haunt me forever, 'Babaaaaaa!'

Since that day, I have not slept a single night. Every time I close my eyes, her voice comes back to me.

I could not save my Aparna. But you, Rammohan Roy, you can save thousands of such girls. Please... don't let them die like this."

Mahadev Bhattacharya fell at Rammohan's feet, sobbing.

Raja Rammohan Roy rose to his feet. "You have given me strength. I must act. If I don't, who will? If not here, I will go to Britain. I will appeal to the Privy Council. I will make this a punishable crime. That is the only way to stop this barbarity in the name of religion. I promise you."

The rest is history. The battle was long and brutal. The Brahmin society, then the most powerful social force, was united against him. Insults and curses rained down. But Rammohan Roy stood firm, unshaken, like a banyan tree.

He became known as the First Modern Man of India.

Today, the story may sound unreal, yet it was the reality of that time. Every one of us with a young daughter in the family sleeps peacefully knowing she is safe, a safety bought with the sacrifices of reformers like Rammohan Roy, Ishwar Chandra Vidyasagar, and many others.

Reformers rarely enjoy majority support, but ultimately, they support the majority to live in peace. They are the rare blessings who change the destiny of society. They are real peace maker for all.

Sacrifice:

Rishavanand ji often had to face a common question. That question is, how justified sacrifice is, and where it is appropriately applied. People in general do not have a clear understanding of this. In this matter, Rishavanand ji's opinion is truly thought-provoking.

Just as there is joy in receiving something, there is an equal joy in doing something for someone or in giving something up for others. However, this depends on the environment in which a person grows up and the kind of family education they receive. Though this is not absolutely true. It is often seen that within the same family, one brother or one among siblings may be sacrifice-minded while another may not be. According to many biologists, along with environment and proper parental upbringing, a person's latent genes may also play a role.

There is also the opposite side. If education is not true education, many consider sacrifice to be foolishness. Since this is a rather low and narrow perception, it is better not to dwell much on it.

Sacrifice is seen not only within families but also among neighbours and in workplaces. There have been instances where a less competent employee was on the verge of losing his job, and a more competent colleague from the same department resigned, putting pressure on the company and thereby saving the other's job. Because if the less competent employee lost his job, his family would fall into severe financial hardship. And once unemployed, the chances of finding another job would be slim. On the other hand, the more competent friend might be in a relatively better position. Yet his mindset of sacrifice surpasses many other considerations.

Self-sacrifice for ideals is the greatest form of sacrifice. Because we have only one life, and to live that life without ideals is equivalent to death. Our true happiness, peace, and the ability to lead a healthy life rest on three strong pillars: ideals, ethics, and honesty.

When people become disturbed over small matters, they should remember that those whom they have accepted as ideal men or women in their lives, whom they have placed almost in the position of God, did not have lives filled with comfort. The amount of suffering they endured for their ideals is something we either do not know or, even if we know, we fail to remember. If we truly recall those sacrifices, we will see that our own sufferings are very minor in comparison. Rishavanand ji's examples deeply touch the human heart.

Perhaps we have gone somewhere for a trip and could not find a good hotel or place to stay for the night. Maybe we had to spend the night at a railway station. We feel considerable irritation, do we not? But we forget that while one uncomfortable night unsettles us, **Purushottam Shri Ramji**, out of obedience to his father's command and for the sake of his ideals, spent fourteen years in exile in the forest.

We all know about **Jesus Christ.** For the sake of truth, he sacrificed his life mercilessly but never compromised with falsehood. A radiant example of sacrifice.

Gautam Buddha, though a prince, left his royal palace and went into exile so that he would not compromise with his ideals. After twelve years of severe penance and attaining enlightenment, he spent the rest of his life as a mendicant.

Guru Arjan was the first Sikh martyr. Mughal Emperor Jahangir had him arrested and taken to Lahore. He was subjected to various inhuman tortures, even being made to sit on a burning iron

plate and having hot sand poured over him. Nothing was spared. Yet despite such atrocities, Guru Arjan remained calm and composed and did not deviate from his ideals.

Husayn ibn Ali was the grandson of Muhammad. In 680 CE, at the Battle of Karbala, Husayn ibn Ali and a small group of his family members and followers were surrounded by the forces of the Umayyad ruler Yazid. Despite being vastly outnumbered, Husayn refused to pledge allegiance to what he believed was an unjust rule. He and nearly all the male members of his small camp were killed. Even his young son was martyred. This event is remembered as a powerful stand for justice, truth, and moral integrity in the face of tyranny.

The memory of the physical torture inflicted upon Husayn still lives on through the processions carried out in his name. However, according to Rishavanand ji, the self-inflicted suffering practised by some of his followers during these processions is not justifiable. Nor are similar practices in other religions, such as the widely practised Charak Puja, where some people inflict pain upon their own bodies to demonstrate their devotion to God. In today's age, such acts are entirely unnecessary and misguided.

There is no end to examples of such superhuman sacrifices. **From Mahavira to Mirabai**, their lives too were filled with neglect, disrespect, and suffering. **Swami Vivekananda** had to endure immense physical hardship because of his ideals, which was one of the causes of his untimely death.

One may ask differently, those whom we have placed in the innermost shrine of our hearts as great souls or as divine beings, why did they not protect themselves from such atrocities? One reason is to teach us that sorrow, suffering, and physical adversity are natural parts of life. Since life will never be filled with happiness alone, but will always contain a mixture of sorrow, if we remain calm and composed in times of distress, those painful moments can pass more easily, and life becomes happier. This is the lesson we learn from these events.

Therefore, embrace sacrifice. The constant desire to gain everything while staying away from sacrifice is the primary cause of losing everything. Because happiness is the ultimate goal of life and losing that is, in essence, losing everything despite having everything.

Wealth:

Another reason people adored him was that he never lived like the self-proclaimed godmen of modern times. He never demanded fees, nor did he accept money for his lectures. According to him, his modest needs were easily met by his salary as a professor. His travels and humble accommodations were always arranged by local organisers. He does not need a lot of money to fulfil his desire to spread knowledge among people.

The most pressing question from the audience was inevitable: Does Rishavanand ji believe that wealth can become a roadblock on the path to spirituality and inner peace?

His answer left the audience spellbound.

"Wealth," he said, "is not a hindrance. it is, in fact, a helpful resource on the journey to spirituality, provided it is earned honestly and does not become the obsession of the mind. The problem begins when one starts believing that accumulating wealth is the ultimate goal of life or that the wealth belongs solely to them. After a certain point, one must begin using a part of their wealth for the betterment of humanity, uplifting the underprivileged, alleviating suffering, and eradicating sin from human life. If not, then wealth does not merely become a roadblock only but the person has probably taken the wrong route."

He continued, "One doesn't need to sell their luxury car or property after a heart attack or a lifetime spent chasing money, only to suddenly promote spirituality. That rarely helps anyone. Instead, wealth should be used wisely, not as a roadblock, but as a vehicle to serve others from the beginning. True spirituality lies in consciously and continually improving one's health, wealth, and relationships, making this practice a part of daily life, a lifelong habit, showing empathy and keeping trust in god and expressing it through disciplined worship."

As per Rishavanand ji, the best is the middle path. Neither run behind excess nor live a pitiful life. He refers to Buddha as support for his thought.

Any kind of excess or extreme must be avoided, Lord Gautama Buddha has said this.

He said, any kind of excess or extremity is not good. This idea he explained through his Middle Path philosophy.

He showed that in life, two "extreme" or "excess" paths must be avoided:

The first is the extreme path of indulgence (excess pleasure): this means running excessively behind sensual pleasure, which only leads people to attachment and suffering.

The second is the extreme path of severe asceticism (excess suffering): this means giving too much pain to the body and renouncing all kinds of comfort and ease. Buddha himself walked this path in his own life and realised that it does not help in attaining Nirvana, but instead destroys both physical and mental strength.

Therefore, by saying “Ati" excess is not good, Gautama Buddha meant that life should be lived in balance. neither excessive indulgence, nor excessive renunciation. By following this Middle Path, true peace can be attained.

About Religious Scriptures' Authenticity

One of the major reasons behind Rishavanand ji 's popularity was that he addressed the many questions people had regarding the various teachings of traditional religious scriptures, questions that truth-seeking individuals could neither resolve through their own reasoning nor receive satisfactory answers to from religious gurus.

On the other hand, some who claim to be scientific-minded try to promote arguments based on superficial scientific facts and theories, often reflecting an arrogant attitude. In contrast, Rishavanand ji was candid. Not only candid, he explained the controversial portions of different scriptures in such a way that they seemed acceptable not only to the deeply religious but also to ordinary people.

A common question that revolved in people's minds was whether our religious texts, such as the Gita, the Bible, or the Quran, truly guide us on the right path. Do these scriptures, written thousands of years ago, really have any relevance today? An even greater concern was that these books contain certain ideas that seem unrealistic in the modern age, and that has become a primary cause of doubt.

Rishavanand ji's views on this matter reflected his profound knowledge, yet they were presented straightforwardly. What created the greatest controversy was his clear statement, without fishing in troubled waters, that none of these religious scriptures was written by God or directly spoken by God. They were composed by human beings. However, it must be acknowledged that they were written by socially aware and knowledgeable individuals. In those times, the discipline and faith prescribed by religious scriptures were extremely important for preserving society and culture. Since our ancestors followed these disciplines and thereby brought society forward as an organised collective, we should remain grateful to them, respect their efforts, and uphold their contributions.

The question then arises: how necessary is it to follow these scriptures in the present age? According to Rishavanand ji, it is not necessary at all. A broad-minded person can live as an educated and civilised member of society and contribute positively without strictly following them. However, since society consists of people of different classes and intellectual levels, adherence to these teachings still has its place. But to rigidly accept everything as the literal word of God would be foolish. Over time, the opinions of various sages have enriched or corrupted these texts. Just as a swan separates milk from water and drinks only the milk, leaving the water behind, we too should accept the good aspects and reject what is no longer relevant. That should be the duty of modern humanity, not blind faith, not fear of sin, but acceptance only to the extent that it brings peace to the mind.

As Rishavanand ji travelled from country to country spreading his views, he naturally faced numerous questions. Yet a free-minded person has one advantage: he does not have to search separately for answers to every question. They appear connected, like flowers of different colours strung on a single thread. A few examples:

It is often said that the Bible states the earth is flat. Is that not laughable today? If such a grave mistake exists in a scripture, does it not imply that everything else in it might also be unrealistic?

In response, Rishavanand ji's words unsettled the questioner but were highly resonant. He said that those who raise such questions often try to establish hearsay as logical arguments without having read the Bible themselves. They make no effort to verify. Such statements, often driven by ulterior motives, have spread everywhere like a geometric progression.

In reality, the Bible nowhere explicitly states that the earth is flat. He further explained:

The Bible is largely theological and poetic, not a science textbook.

Certain verses, such as "Four corners of the earth," "The ends of the earth," and "The earth is fixed and cannot be moved," have led people to that interpretation.

Even if minor inaccuracies exist, should we not focus instead on the countless noble teachings within the Bible and practise them?

Another frightening claim is that, according to the Quran, killing non-believers is a virtuous act. According to Rishavanand ji , such statements were written in the context of historical conflicts, but educated Muslims of today do not interpret them that way.

Being Muslim does not mean one must follow every word of the Quran literally. That itself is proof. The Quran contains many things that may not be suitable for the modern age and may seem harsh or outdated beyond the boundaries of time and law.

Extremist groups ignore context and weaponised selective verses, but mainstream Islamic scholarship treats them as historically situated.

For these reasons, religious scriptures cannot be considered divine compositions or literal utterances of God. They were written by human beings and therefore reflect the shadows of different historical moments.

He illustrated this with examples: From the Bible: "An eye for an eye," "stoning for adultery," "women must remain silent in church."
From the Quran: "Cutting off the hand of a thief," "polygamy (up to four wives)."

In today's world, only the uneducated or extremely rigid individuals attempt to follow such directives literally. It is practically impossible, as they contradict the civil laws and civic sense of most countries.

Similarly, dress codes prescribed by religions were suitable for the climate and health conditions of particular regions and times. The clothing appropriate for the 40-degree Celsius heat of the Arabian desert cannot be suitable for sub-zero temperatures elsewhere. Likewise, face-covering garments may pose security concerns in modern contexts. People have now come to understand this. Head covering is vanishing day by day in modern cities.

In his view, the least flawed among the scriptures is the Gita, though astonishingly it was composed centuries before the Bible or the Quran. At the same time, Rishavanand ji cautioned that since everyone tends to consider their own religion the best, it is natural that, being initiated into Hinduism, he would regard the Gita as supreme. Yet he elaborated extensively on why he and many intellectuals believe the Gita offers the most balanced guidance for life, and also on which of its aspects may not be fully practicable.

For example, in Chapter 3, Verse 37 of the Bhagavad Gita, Lord Krishna says to Arjuna that these six inherent characteristics of human beings are the reason for unhappiness: Kāma (Desire / Lust), Krodha (Anger), Lobha (Greed), Moha (Delusion / Attachment), Mada (Pride / Arrogance), Matsarya (Envy / Jealousy). Therefore, one should restrain them. A beautiful and valuable teaching, without doubt.

If we think deeply, we see that mental unrest, fear, and anxiety arise from one or more of these six passions. Yet do people truly eliminate them? No, because religious teachers often present them as absolutes. This creates doubt about their practical relevance. Is a life without desire truly intended? Creation and continuation of life itself depend on desire.

Should anger be completely abandoned? Then should one remain silent in the face of injustice? Is greed not sometimes a natural reaction? How can attachment be entirely removed? The sweet bond among family members is itself an attachment. True, attachment causes restlessness and anxiety, but a life without attachment would resemble that of the dead.

In conclusion, Rishavanand ji emphasises that these six passions have been exaggerated. The Gita does not demand their total eradication for all; rather, it advises that they should not dominate the mind. Complete renunciation may not be possible, but they must be controlled. For those who have embraced monastic life, striving for total renunciation may be the ideal.

From all these discussions and critiques, it becomes clear that although the Gita is one of the world's oldest scriptures, it remains profoundly relevant today.

Finally, Rishavanand ji 's closing advice is worth echoing: do not force belief, nor reject others' beliefs; accept one, accept all, or accept none. But regard both believers and non-believers with equal respect. Fighting, violence, and revenge have no connection with religion. Every scripture ultimately teaches love and righteousness. If we follow only that central message, life will indeed become beautiful.

Lastly, Rishavanand ji said, "I am not here to say what is right and what is wrong. I am here to guide you to the right path of truth and joy. What I have described from different angles is how to live life. My advice is this: you may follow one religion, or you may follow all religions. Following rcligion does not mean performing rituals, but learning from the scriptures how to lead a beautiful life for oneself and one's family, where family is not limited to relatives but, in a broader sense, includes society. Having deeply studied almost all religions, from the most ancient Bon religion of Tibet to the relatively recent Islam and Sikhism, I can advise you on the ten top principles that everyone should follow. You may go to a temple, mosque, church, or gurdwara and join in chanting, which brings solace; but in real life, follow these ten."

He also said, "Before that, I want to discuss something about religions, as most people are not aware of religions other than their own. Even if they know, they often know the wrong things. It is very important to have complete information, and an informed decision is always better than an ignorant action.

Many think that Hinduism is the oldest religion, especially in the Indian subcontinent. It is not entirely true. There is no single, universally agreed-upon oldest religion. According to available and widely accepted research, animism and Bon in Tibet existed thousands of years ago, long before written history. Bon was based on nature worship, ritual healing, and spirit beliefs. Later, a new religion took birth in Tibet called Buddhism, which became very popular and spread across many countries.

Then, where does Hinduism stand? According to historians and researchers, Hinduism is the oldest major organised religion still widely practised today. Its roots go back to the Vedic tradition (around 1500 BC or earlier) and possibly to the Indus Valley Civilisation (around 2500 BC or older, though debated).

What about Christianity? Christianity began in the 1st century CE, after the crucifixion of Jesus, and is therefore approximately 2,000 years old. Some experts say that widespread institutional following of Christianity began about three hundred years after his death.

Islam (7th century CE) was founded in the 600s AD and now has nearly 2 billion followers. Sikhism (15th century CE) was founded in the 1400s AD in Punjab and today has over 25 million followers.

I often discuss this because, to understand the core of a religion's teaching, people should have knowledge of history, as religion is not science but a history-based social system.

Now, I want to suggest the ten principles one should follow irrespective of whether they go to a church, mosque, or temple. You need not read all the scriptures yourself, as I have extracted these principles from them, filtering out the parts that may not be suitable for today's time.

1. Love and Compassion for Others

The Bible teaches, 'Love your neighbour as yourself.'

The Quran emphasises mercy and kindness. The Gita encourages seeing the divine in all beings.
All three remind us that hatred divides, but love unites.
Swami Vivekananda said, 'The highest truth is the human being; there is nothing above humanity.'

2. Truthfulness

Truth is sacred in every scripture. The Bible condemns false witness. The Quran commands believers to stand firmly for the truth. The Gita values honesty as a divine quality. A truthful person builds trust; a dishonest one destroys it.

3. Charity and Helping the Poor

Charity is central in all three traditions. The Quran makes charity (zakat) a duty. The Bible praises generosity toward the needy.
The Gita teaches selfless giving without

expecting reward.
Helping the less fortunate purifies the heart.

4. Forgiveness

The Bible strongly promotes forgiveness, even forgiving enemies.
The Quran teaches that forgiving others brings divine reward.
The Gita promotes letting go of anger and resentment.
Forgiveness frees the soul more than revenge ever could.

5. Self-Control

The Gita teaches mastery over the mind and senses.
The Bible speaks about resisting temptation.
The Quran emphasizes discipline, especially through fasting.
A person who controls themselves cannot easily be controlled by circumstances.

6. Faith and Trust in God

All three scriptures teach surrender to the Divine will.
Faith gives strength during hardship.

Whether called God, Allah, or Bhagavan, trust in a higher power brings inner peace.

7. Justice and Fairness

The Quran repeatedly stresses justice, even if it is against oneself. The Bible teaches fairness and righteousness.
The Gita encourages acting according to dharma (righteous duty). A just society begins with just individuals.

8. Patience in Difficult Times

The Quran praises those who are patient.
The Bible teaches endurance during trials. The Gita advises remaining steady in success and failure. Patience turns suffering into strength.

9. Responsibility for One's Actions

The Gita teaches karma; every action has consequences. The Bible speaks of reaping what one sows. The Quran says every soul is accountable for its deeds.

Blaming others weakens us; responsibility strengthens us.

10. Gratitude

All three scriptures encourage thankfulness.

Gratitude creates contentment. A grateful heart is rarely bitter. This echoes the story I often tell about young Naren explaining to his teacher, through the example of the non-existence of cold and darkness.

All these are not superficial things to follow, but part of inner transformation. Until inner transformation takes place within, all rituals and guidelines remain hollow words to a person.

The Bible, the Quran, and the Bhagavad Gita may differ in theology, stories, and historical context, but their moral teachings often converge on universal human values."

Rishavanand ji concluded in one sentence, "The real question is not which book is greater. The real question is: are we practising the good that is already written in them?"

Social counterattack:

Nothing is absolute in this world; fame often invites shadows. As Rishavanand ji's popularity soared, a few critics emerged, driven by jealousy and suspicion. They began whispering about his intentions. "He's just building his brand," they claimed. "Soon, he'll be like all the others, milking his popularity, charging fees, chasing luxury."

They were convinced that sooner or later, he would start accepting money or demanding money even for all his activities, which other famous gurus often follow.

They had no idea that Rishavanand ji was preparing for something far more powerful than what anyone could anticipate, sitting backstage for his best-ever performance, which is beyond anyone's thought.

One of the volunteers of the mayor's program came to the room and called him,

"Sir, everyone has arrived and is waiting for you to come on stage to start the program."

Rishavanand ji realised he had been so deep in thought, recalling his last decade's journey, that he forgot he was the most honourable guest at today's event. He felt a bit excited when he heard that one of the richest industrialists in the country, commonly known as MK, had come to attend the program. MK had become his follower over the last several years. MK also wanted to establish an ashram for him anywhere on earth, but Rishavanand ji humbly declined many times his proposal of gifting him something or other.

Despite his demanding schedule, MK would often make time to visit Rishavanand ji. Over time, Rishavanand ji came to see that MK was a kind-hearted man, unlike many others with wealth. He is someone who truly walks the talk, and that sincerity made Rishavanand ji feel uplifted in his company. Yet, Rishavanand ji remained grounded in his own view of the world, seeing everyone, regardless of status, as a child of the Divine, and nothing more or less.

On the dais, several dignitaries, including the mayor and the minister, delivered their speeches. Who could ignore the richest industrialist who came on his own? It was a surprise for all. So, the organisers called MK to speak briefly about Rishavanand ji. As per his nature, MK explained how he got impressed after watching one lecture of Rishavanand ji, how he came closer to him, and why he rushed to meet him whenever Rishavanand ji came to the country.

In the end, he shared that true peace would only come to his heart if he could assist Rishavanand ji and support his noble mission. He was willing to offer anything, should Rishavanand ji be open to accepting it. But time and again, Rishavanand ji had humbly declined his generous proposals. To ease the mood before Rishavanand ji began his serious discourse, he quipped with a playful smile, 'I seek the blessing of helping you, but you are not helping me, accepting my help!' The remark drew gentle laughter, softening the moment with wit and sincerity.

The hall's walls seemed about to break from the applause when Rishi stood in front of the microphone. Media cameras were ready to capture something new. Rishi was known for doing or saying something new each time. So, every lecture of his became breaking news globally and boosted TRPs for media houses. However, no one expected what Rishavanand ji said that day.

A pin-drop silence spread over the hall, followed by some whispering. The reason: Rishavanand ji accepted MK's proposal and demanded not just anything, but one million dollars. He also refused to give his talk that day and requested everyone to come the next day when he would speak at length, and would probably be his last lecture.

True Revenge:

It was indeed big news in the newspapers the next day. The media started scolding Rishavanand ji from the very moment it was broadcast live:

"Godman or greedy man? Nation wants to know".

"The mask wiped out."

"See the real face."

"The greatest marketer selling his brand at a high price."

The mayor's expectation was right that the entire world would be eager to see what Rishi would say the next day. So, he shifted the program to a nearby small stadium. Many social and political organisations gathered there to show him black flags, marking him a fake, greedy guru.

The stadium was overfilled. Rishavanand ji came with high-security arrangements for the first time in his life at the request of the local police headquarters. They didn't want to take any chances of being in the news for the wrong reason if someone insulted or assaulted him. An unknown old man was the only one accompanying Rishavanand ji.

Rishavanand ji started delivering his lecture. "Yes, I have dedicated my life to the service and well-being of humanity. Yes, I had never accepted money, not until yesterday. But the past is not limited to the last ten years. There is a deeper past, a past before the past, that most of you, my dear followers, know nothing about. And what many fail to see is that everything comes at a cost. The journey that shaped who I am today carries a price that no sum, millions or otherwise, can truly repay.

Just as you cannot measure the sacrifice of your mother in money, yet you still try to honour it by gifting something great to your mother, that is how it should be. So, what I asked is not a fee, but an acknowledgement, an offering to the path that made me. It was a tight slap on my face by this unknown old man, you see, sitting on the stage."

Rishavanand ji turned back, held the old man's hand, and brought him to the front. "He is the man who taught me why I should not live a bitch-life. His one slap and one curse helped me live a godly life rather than the bitch-life I originally deserved. It helped all of you to get me and find a new direction toward life, religion, and happiness. He is the man who helped and supported my family for years as the younger brother of my father. He is the man who sold his only asset, a small Ambassador car, to arrange the marriages of my sisters.

If you agree that I have been doing good for society, then it is virtually his sacrifice for society that cannot be repaid. However, I wanted to give him something that would attract the attention of the entire world, the best of the best gift. People should remember this event as the core of a religion that teaches us to sacrifice to do good for others, out of love and compassion, without any expectation."

A car rolled in front of the stage. MK came out of the car and went onto the stage.

He handed over the key to the old man standing beside Rishavanand ji. MK said, "Rishavanand ji is completely greedless and an ocean of ultimate knowledge. This is the Ferrari the monk bought with the one million dollars he accepted from me yesterday. Rishi gifted the car to his uncle, the old man, who virtually transformed a tenth-standard dropout into the great Rishavanand ji. And rest assured, Rishavanand ji will remain the same as before, devoted to mankind, and we shall continue to receive his blessings and direction to live a better life always."

The best of the best revenge, best of the best message, people shall remember it as they remember the Ferrari over all other superior things.

Avulsion

As usual, Rishavanand ji's talk in his own city, where he was born and brought up, the Ferrari incident spread across the world like an inferno. His mailbox was flooded with praise and invitations. However, as expected, he delivered yet another twist in his next declaration that shocked the world: he was no longer going to give any talks anywhere. He wants to live a simple life like other people do and wants to devote in to research to deliver something bigger to society.

Many people raised the question: how can he, as a monk, be a simple man, a scientist, or live a family life? Rishavanand ji's response was simple: "I have never claimed to be a monk, nor does our ashram require it. Our ashram follows a simple philosophy: to work for mankind and uplift human lives. That is what I intend to do."

He also added, "Swami Vivekananda did not begin his spiritual journey as a monk. He was not even a Brahmin, just as I am not. He was born with an exceptional intellect and wisdom, cultivated them, and dedicated his life to the betterment of people. Yes, he formally took monastic vows after the death of his spiritual guru, Ramakrishna Paramahamsa, and lived as a sannyasi (renunciate). But people remember him not merely because he was a sannyasi, but for his extraordinary contributions in revitalising Hindu philosophy.

I, too, will live a family life, and that does not conflict with my thoughts, work, or the wisdom I aim to offer to the world. Attire or its colour has nothing to do with wisdom."

The reason he explained was that whatever he wanted to convey had already been done. Truly, there wasn't much more to say when it came to the philosophy of life. Other celebrities continue speaking either because they have nothing else to do or simply to fulfil their dream of becoming wealthy. Neither of these applied to him.

As a pure scientist of biology, he could now concentrate on basic biological research to contribute something truly phenomenal, something people can't even imagine in today's world. Also, why waste time travelling to deliver the same philosophy when technology can do that? His lectures and books could be freely distributed and used to attract more people to his philosophical wisdom.

Rishavanand ji joined a leading government research institute in Delhi, and he became known as Dr. Rishi. From the most junior staff to the senior scientists and even the director, everyone at the institute was proud to have such a remarkable philosopher and globally respected monk among them. Beyond his philosophical work, his PhD research earned him numerous accolades, recognising him as a scientist with a truly unique perspective. True to form, within a couple of years, he had already published several groundbreaking papers, including in prestigious journals like Science and Nature, an accomplishment many scientists only dream of achieving in their entire careers, at least once, but the majority fail to attain that height.

Dr. Rishi's co-author on all his publications and his colleague, scientist Dr. Megha, was one of the key pillars in helping him settle into the traditional research environment, a space often filled with jealousy and rivalry, which began to surface as soon as Dr. Rishi started gaining recognition and became the talk of the town. The reason behind it is Dr. Rishi came from an environment where empathy, cooperation, and working for others were his guiding principles.

Rishi and Megha often sat together for long hours discussing scientific matters and many other topics. Rishi was deeply impressed by Megha's knowledge, intellect, and dedication. Megha's warm and pleasing personality created a sense of affection and admiration in his heart.

On the other hand, Megha was equally moved, so much so that he felt he could do anything for Rishi, whom he admired the most. Her heart filled with joy whenever she spoke to Rishi or worked with him in the lab. Though they maintained a respectful physical distance, their minds and souls were boundless and unconfined. They became close friends. As Megha was only a little younger than Rishi, they began addressing each other by name.

One day, Rishi and Megha were working late, completing an important experiment. Rishi had no car; he led a simple life, so Megha offered, "Should I drop you somewhere today, wherever you're headed?"

Rishi replied, "That would be nice if you don't mind. Please drop me near INA Market. I assume you're going toward Noida?"

Megha smiled, "Come on, get in."

They walked to the parking lot and got into the car. The conversation flowed deeply between them. Suddenly, Rishi noticed that they had passed INA long ago and were now nearing South Extension.

"Oh Megha, look, we've reached South Extension! I was supposed to get down at INA," Rishi suddenly exclaimed.

Megha pressed the brake and parked near the metro station. "Sorry, Rishi. My apologies. I completely forgot; we were so caught up in conversation. Should I take you back to INA?"
"No, that's not needed. I'll take the metro from here, it's just a few stops away. Bye," Rishi said with a wave and walked toward the metro station.

Time flows faster than we realise, especially when spent with someone you truly enjoy being with. Within a short time, Rishi and Megha were no longer strangers. They became each other's most trustworthy companions, often going out of their way to help one another.

People started believing they were in love.

One day, Rishi joked, "Hey, remember the early days? You once gave me a lift to INA."

Megha smiled, "Not INA, boss! I dropped you at South Extension. Your memory is weak!"

"Yes, yes. That's what I meant," Rishi laughed. "But you know what? I was enjoying our conversation so much that I passed INA knowingly and didn't tell you to stop."

Megha looked at him meaningfully, "And do you think that while I was driving, I didn't realise we had passed INA? Then guess why I didn't stop?

Rishi smiled, "Well, here's another surprise, I had no plan to go to INA that day. I had no meeting, no friend to see. I just wanted to spend some time with my most important colleague, so I made up the story. After you dropped me at South Extension, I booked a cab and went back to the lab for some urgent work."

"Oh! You never told me this before, you little cheater," Megha laughed. "Then here's one for you, dear boss. That day, I wasn't going to Noida either. I was supposed to go to my mother's house in Rohini, which is in the opposite direction! After dropping you, I took a U-turn at the next crossing. Can you guess why?"

Such little moments brought them closer. But it didn't last forever. Dr. Megha got an excellent opportunity to work at the National Institutes of Health (NIH) in the United States for two years. At first, she refused. Rishi sensed that she might miss this major opportunity and global recognition just because she didn't want to leave him alone.

Rishi urged her, "It's just two years, Megha. You must go."

But Megha snapped, "No. I don't want fame or name. I'm fine here."

"Why not, why not?" Rishi asked, clearly upset.

"Do you really want to know why?" she shouted. "If I go, you won't be able to survive here for a single day. I know that your colleagues have already started conspiring against you out of jealousy. You are not made for this world; you were raised in a puritan environment."

But who could overpower Rishi? His logic, his wisdom, and his deep vision had the power to mesmerise. Eventually, Megha had to go.

She wasn't wrong. Rishi soon began to realise the shift. Those who once admired him turned against him. His research projects started getting rejected one after another. Whispers spread that he was more interested in supernatural studies than in real science.

Rishi began to lose patience day by day.

The situation reached its peak when he was called in for a very high-level meeting at the Department of Biotechnology. He found prominent scientists from across India present at that meeting. The reason?

The project Dr. Rishi submitted was beyond anyone's imagination. The committee gave him a chance to express his thoughts and explain how he planned to proceed. Because the project was about discovering LIFE or the SOUL, and recreating it physically through biological reactions. Biology, till today, has only imagined growing or transforming one cell into another. Not a single scientist has yet created an artificial cell. And here was Dr. Rishi, demanding funding to create Life.

Some scientists expressed their views that Dr Rishi lacks the qualities of a real scientist, and that he was proposing something absurd just to float above others. Others argued that since hundreds of scientists in India waste government money without producing anything significant, no practical implications, no translational research, the government should support someone like Dr. Rishi, instead of bossing him.

The committee asked Dr. Rishi to explain his plan in detail. Dr. Rishi flatly refused, fearing that his idea might be stolen, which was very common. An idea is the most valuable asset of a scientist, and it is unethical to force someone to reveal it before making any progress. The committee members were not happy with his refusal to disclose the core of his research. So, not only did they reject his project, but they also advised him to concentrate on something more practical.

The last comment echoed in his ears just like the slap from his uncle two decades ago: "Dr. Rishi, everything costs money: your lab, your students, even your institute-provided quarters. You're wasting government funds. So, please think about it and do something practical, just like what all other scientists across India are doing."

A thin smile appeared on Dr. Rishi's lips. He stood up and began walking toward the door. The committee members heard a murmur slip through his smiling lips: "Oh my God! what all the other scientists are doing…all the other scientists are doing….all others…".

No one saw Dr. Rishi in his office after that day. After several days, they checked his quarters. Bijan, his cook, an old man from a remote village of Uttarakhand who lived with him, said that Dr. Rishi had left everything as it was about a week ago and had not returned since.

As usual, Bijan was speaking with him the evening before, during dinner. He had asked, "Sir, you've been looking disturbed for the last few days. What's the matter?"

Dr. Rishi replied, "You're right. I am finding these research centres like jungles, where quality doesn't matter, only political power. People are impure. No discipline."

Bijan didn't like the comment, as he was from a forest region himself. He protested, "Sir, don't blame the jungle as a place without discipline. Everything in a jungle is the most disciplined and pure."

Dr Rishi stopped eating and raised his face. He looked into Bijan's eyes, and slowly, his gaze travelled millions of miles. He told

Brijan jokingly, "Then let us go to the jungle and laughed aloud."

A few days later, Bijan also left the quarters. Neither of them ever returned.

PART 2

Fifth Dimensions

The sky gradually turned deep blue. Manish hadn't noticed when the clouds had drifted far away below his feet. Along the horizon stood the still, radiant mountain ranges. Beyond them, Leha, Tibet. Beneath the satin layer of white clouds, a green carpet spread out. At sixteen thousand feet above, he eased the engine power from full throttle.

Now, some time just drifting. Routine flight practice. Along with the surveillance of the border adjacent to Tibet. Below, though faint, he could see the villages of Chitkul, Rakcham and Sangla.

He had spent a few months in ground training there, during the early days after joining the Air Force. Only for a little longer would human settlements be visible. After that, uninhabited deep forests and mountain ranges. After circling like this for about half an hour, he would return to base.

The afternoon was turning into evening. The sun leaned westward. Unrestrained, sharp rays dazzled his eyes. He thought of putting on his sunglasses. As he reached out to get them, his eyes fell on a particular section of the dashboard, a sight that would send a chill down any pilot's spine. The red light marked REFA was blinking rapidly. Right engine fire alarm.

Manish swiftly turned around to look at the engine. There was no visible fire, but black smoke was coming out. He immediately decided to return to base. He neutralised the right engine and took a 180-degree turn.

He kept glancing nervously at the engine, sensing imminent danger. The warning light continued blinking. Even repeated resets didn't work. He didn't have to wait long. Within two minutes, the fear turned into reality. Flames began to emerge from the right engine.

He turned on the extinguisher. It didn't work. Within moments, the entire rear section of the aircraft was engulfed in flames. To return to base, Manish would need to fly at least another twenty to twenty-five minutes. So, he did what is considered a pilot's last duty: release the lock and push eject. In a flash, the glass canopy above slid back. He was ejected with the seat, rising nearly fifty feet. He saw the pilotless burning aircraft zooming ahead at great speed. In a short while, it disappeared into the kingdom of clouds.

Even in this moment of extreme crisis, fate did not abandon him. As he descended swiftly, suddenly he realised something still positive. The parachute attached to the pilot's seat deployed at the right time. Above his head, the massive canopy seemed like the protective palm of a blessing.

His speed slowed. Floating in the air, he descended downward. Below was dense jungle. As far as the eye could see, no sign of human life. And dusk was setting in. Even if he survived the fall, there was little assurance he'd return safely to base.

Manish remembered Captain Mathur. During training, he used to give examples, saying, *No matter how dire the situation, until the last breath, one must assume the chance of survival is one hundred per cent.* That gave him strength.

He controlled the parachute and landed near a mountain river. At least he'd get drinking water. And it would give him a hint of which direction to go. A river is a best friend in a dense forest, nourishing and guiding those who have lost, as the river ultimately flows through the habitat before finally reaching to its destination, the ocean. However, it wouldn't be wise to move any further today. The tall trees had already blocked the last light of the sun. Though there was still light in the sky, the ground was dark.

He decided to climb a tree and spend the night there. He had to prepare himself for a tough fight. In the rush of the crash, he hadn't been able to contact Basecamp either. It might take them a few days just to locate the aircraft. Even that might be pointless, because the plane could've crashed fifty to sixty miles away. In this dense forest, that distance was massive.

He washed his face and hands in the icy-cold water of the river. Drank water till he was full. That would be his only meal tonight. He climbed a tall but slim pine tree. Unfastened his belt and tied himself to a branch.

Slowly, darkness thickened. And with it came the occasional cries of nocturnal birds. The chirping of crickets. Manish started thinking of home. Of his father, mother. His younger sister Jhuma who is just two years younger than Manish. His elder sister, who was a renowned scientist but left her job, returned to the village and engaged herself in the betterment of downtrodden people and also engaged herself in teaching in a local school. They didn't know what he was going through. If they did, their hearts would break in pain. Compared to that, his pain is nothing.

Tomorrow will be the day Jhuma's Ph.D. viva. She must be terribly anxious. It would have been nice to call her today and give her courage. Surely, he would've said, *"Don't worry, my lovely sister, I'm always beside you."* Again, he remembered Captain Mathur. He used to say, *"In times of grave danger, think only of yourself. If you start thinking of loved ones, the mind will weaken. That won't help you, nor your loved ones."*

Manish braced himself. Better to think about what he needed to do tomorrow. If possible, he must get a few hours of sleep too.

It must have been a no-moon night. The sky was filled with stars. Only then did he realise that stars also shine with light, and the lights are really bright in a pitch-dark environment. Through the gaps between trees in the jungle, fireflies blinked on and off. After staring into the jungle for some time, suddenly his heart skipped a beat. Among the blinking lights, one seemed to glow steadily. Could it be? Surely someone must be there.

His eyes kept returning to that light again and again.

Yes, it was really glowing steadily.

Research Centre:

Without even realising it, the night passed by just like that. A faint red hue appeared in the eastern sky. At the crack of dawn, Manish climbed down from the tree. He started walking in the direction where he had seen that light.

After trekking through the forest for about half an hour, he spotted a small house. Made of stones stacked on top of one another. The roof was a wooden gable, quite sturdy. Large trees surrounding the house probably kept it hidden from above.

As he moved closer, he saw not one, but two houses. Both were of the same type, yet stood apart from each other. When he reached the front, he saw no one. Both houses were locked. Had someone once lived here? Perhaps not anymore. The little hope that had flickered in his heart dimmed with apprehension. Suddenly, a baritone voice rang out behind him, clear and confident. "Who are you, young man?"

Manish turned around and saw a middle-aged man standing there, dressed in a long white gown like that of a church father. His skin and build suggested middle age, but his long grey beard made him appear older, almost monk-like. Manish hadn't noticed when or from where the man had arrived.

In moments like this, he remembered what Mr. Mathur had taught him: *"I am Manish. I serve India. And I have not come to do any harm."*

A man stepped forward. He smiled slightly and put a hand on Manish's shoulder. "I am not afraid, my boy. Come with me," he said.

He started walking toward the northern house. The house, which had looked big from the outside, didn't feel that big once they entered. One reason could be that everything the gentleman needed to live was inside this one room, a bed cum kitchen cum a store. To Manish's surprise, the man spoke in clear Bengali: "From your name, I can tell you're Bengali. And judging by your attire, looks like you serve the country. So, what brings you to this jungle?"

In his excitement, Manish blurted out, "You're Bengali!" The gentleman turned to him and said, "As far as I know, discipline is your first lesson. So, answer my question first, then ask yours."

There was something hypnotic in his gaze. One by one, Manish narrated all the events since yesterday afternoon.

The man listened quietly. Then, after a pause, he said, "My name is Rishi. However, neither am I a priest nor a Rishi (Monk) in the real sense anymore. I am just a scientist. And a scientist in a jungle means good for nothing, you can simply conclude."

Manish realised that he looked serious, but had a beautiful sense of humour. Which, as Rishi had noticed, was common among all truly intelligent persons.

As Manish was wondering what to say, the gentleman continued, "Spent my childhood in a remote village in Bengal. Then I travelled around various countries. Could never settle down anywhere. Finally chose to shift my research in this remote jungle. Of course, before coming here, I lived in Delhi for about two and a half years and worked in a well-known research institute."

Suddenly, it struck Manish. He asked, "Sir, are you the famous Rishavanand ji? We read in the newspaper that you suddenly vanished from a research centre in Delhi. There was a lot of breaking news and many predictions about your sudden disappearance. I also knew many things about you from someone."

He gave an affirmative nod of his head. He asked, "Someone? Who is that someone?"

Manish went into deep thought. His eyes started glittering. A happy feeling appeared in his face. Observing Manish's silence, Dr Rishi asked, "What are you thinking, young man. Anything serious you find in it?"

Manish replied in short, "That I shall tell you later, I do not like to disturb your focus from your research right now. But tell me, Sir, why are you here? What are you doing here?"

"No need to call me 'Sir.' You can call me a scientist because I believe scientists have no caste, religion, age or vanity of their qualification or position. They have only one identity, that they are scientists. One identity, one task: to create something new, to give something new to the world. Though it is unfortunately the other way around in our country. Though 'scientist' is a bit of a clunky word. You may call me Dr. Rishi."

"So, you're a scientist. But in this jungle…?"

"This jungle is the ideal place for research. Surprised? In your world of bricks, cement, dust, smoke, politics, TA, DA, accounts, and audits, true scientific pursuit is impossible. Audit, oh my god! Some stupid people treat us like grocery shop employees, 'that is cheap, this is expensive, why did you buy expensive, what is your intention?' Sometimes I felt like saying, 'My immediate intention is to give you a tight slap.' Anyway, it is a problem of our system, so why should I blame an individual? Also, why should I blame the system at all, as many scientists are more focused on earning money by wrong deed than innovation," he laughed. "So, I left that jungle, which is called research institutes, and settled here to worship the god of creativity through my work."

Observing Manish's silence, he asked, "I've travelled all the major cities of the world. You can't dismiss my experience as trivial."

"No, I'm not saying that. Nor do I have the right to. But… what are you researching here? Plants?" Manish replied promptly.

He was silent and then spoke in a deep voice, "Life!", as if the sounds were coming out of his heart, not his mouth.

"Life?" Manish asked, full of surprise.

"Exactly. Not much time left. The whole world will see. I will push science ahead by at least two hundred years."

Manish couldn't make any sense of it. So, he interrupted, "I really don't understand. Could you please explain a little?"

Dr. Rishi looked at him. He observed Manish carefully and then said, "You probably didn't get anything to eat last night. Let's have some breakfast first."

It was true. But Manish had become so fascinated by Dr. Rishi's words that he didn't feel any hunger or thirst. Being a student of science, he naturally felt a strong curiosity.

While eating, Dr. Rishi said that after breakfast, Manish should take a bath. At exactly nine o'clock, they'd head to the laboratory.

Manish went to his washroom and found it well equipped. A pipe brought flowing spring water all day long. Wearing one of Dr. Rishi's spare sets of clothes, Manish stood before the laboratory and found the door open.

That meant Dr. Rishi had already gone in. He checked his wrist watch, it was five past nine. He felt a bit awkward. The gentleman followed such strict discipline that even a soldier would be embarrassed.

Upon entering the room, Manish found it fairly dark as light was coming through a small window on the eastern side of the room. Right in the centre, one table and two chairs.

Dr. Rishi sat on a chair, writing something in a thick notebook. He gestured for Manish to sit on a stool placed nearby. Sitting down, he began to observe the surroundings carefully. There was a large door on one side, the only entrance. On the right and left walls were long tables, each packed with various instruments. Some of the instruments were familiar to Manish, but most were not. The wall opposite the door held a massive device. It looked something like a large electrical panel. Covered with countless switches, meters, and indicators.

Until now, Manish had thought an aircraft's dashboard was the most complicated thing, but now he realised, compared to this machine, the dashboard was just a fraction. The machine was quite deep, at least eight to ten feet.

After about ten minutes of focused writing, Dr. Rishi looked up. Taking off his glasses and placing them on the table, he said, "Do you know what I was writing? What I did yesterday and what I'll do today. In this notebook, I've recorded every single detail of my invention. Even if I don't live to see tomorrow, this notebook will push science two hundred years ahead."

Running his hand gently over the notebook, he added, "It's the epic of science."

Manish said, "You were going to explain your invention to me."

Dr. Rishi smiled and said, "Yes, yes. But how much you'll understand, I don't know. So, I'll start from the beginning. I'll ask you some questions. Just answer honestly. If you don't know, just say so."

"All right. Ask me," Manish replied.

"Have you seen a photocopy machine?"

Manish hadn't expected the first question from such a great scientist to be this simple. He replied, "Yes, Xerox."

Dr. Rishi said, "Up to the 'Yes,' you were right. But the next part is wrong. 'Xerox' is actually the name of a company that first patented the photocopier. Out of ignorance, people call all photocopiers 'Xerox.' So, I've corrected your mistake first.

A copy machine reads the colour and brightness of every minuscule part of the original document; this is called scanning.

Then it places those same colours and brightness levels at the exact corresponding positions on another piece of paper, done. When you look at it all together, it seems like the same picture or text.

These are two-dimensional, meaning they have length and width. Now, imagine a machine that could make a three-dimensional copy. That means length, width, and depth."

Suddenly, Manish remembered Tintin's friend, Professor Calculus. He had tried to invent a 3D copying machine and ended up in trouble with Rastapopoulos and company. But Manish didn't mention that to Dr. Rishi. Instead, he showed interest and said, "If you could explain a bit more clearly."

"I will, I will. You'll understand everything."

Dr. Rishi asked to borrow Manish's 'asta-dhatu' (eight-metals) ring. Taking it in his hand, he said, "This object of your blind faith and superstition will help me demonstrate the concept."

Dr. Rishi said, "There's one more thing. The bonding between those atoms also matters. That's why the machine includes provisions for pressure, heat, and catalysts. The data, for what to apply and where, is already stored in this machine. You could call this the fourth dimension. So?"

"I've heard of the fourth dimension before," Manish stated proudly.

"That's a different concept. What we're talking about here is pure physics, while Einstein's fourth dimension was time. This is something entirely different, a new idea."

Manish jumped out of his chair. Such a simple idea, how had no one thought of it before? If this were possible, then anything in the world could be duplicated!

Dr. Rishi said, "This was the part I couldn't get anyone to understand. For many years, I kept submitting this project. Again and again, it was rejected as the rantings of a madman. But come on, outside the 118 elements of the periodic table, nothing else exists in the universe. Trees, soil, cars, horses, humans, everything is just different combinations of those 118 elements. The main complexity was in creating the right environment, meaning the biochemical reactions and perfect bonding. That's what I finally achieved after all these years."

"Then why haven't you published this yet?" Manish asked.

"I will, I will. Just a little bit left. Once that's done, I'll go public. Anyway, enough talk. Let me show you the result of my madness."

Dr. Rishi took the ring and went to the machine. He pulled out a drawer labelled 'Source' and placed the ring inside. Then he flipped several switches. He turned on the computers placed on both sides. He spent about four or five minutes doing something on the computers. Then he took the ring out of the drawer and handed it back to Manish, saying, "The analysis is done. But production will take about an hour. This one's quite complex. It's nearly eleven o'clock. Come on, let's prepare lunch. After lunch, we'll return and see the results."

Lunch consisted of rice and boiled greens. Dr. Rishi said, "This is enough for me. Young man, it might be a bit difficult for you, but manage with it for now. It's just a matter of a day. Tomorrow afternoon, two or three people will come here from a distant tribal village. They bring me food and necessary supplies in exchange for a bit of money. I'll send you back with them."

Manish asked, "How far do I have to go from here to find human habitation?"

"Oh, it's quite far. If you leave tomorrow afternoon, you'll reach the next morning. But there's nothing to fear. They know the roads well and are very trustworthy. They won't let any harm come to you."

"No, I'm not worried. But tell me something, how did you manage to do all this in such a remote place?"

"That's a long story. Before coming here, I worked at a reputed research centre in Delhi, which I already told you. But as I said, they thought I was crazy. I didn't get any funding. So, I decided to leave everything behind and work on my own. Fortunately, I had inherited a good amount of ancestral property. I never got married, and after spending many years abroad, I lost contact with my close relatives. So, I sold everything and came here. After many years of effort, I built this laboratory. At first, I had two or three salaried assistants. One by one, they all left. Who wants to stay in this wilderness? I came here with my cook, Bijan, who used to stay with me at the research centre quarters. In fact, I learned many things about the jungle from him. He not only inspired me to come here but also accompanied me, as he loved the jungle. He was the one who helped me do all these things. Without him, I couldn't have managed anything in this remote place.

However, he became too old, and for proper medical care, I sent him back to his native place, which is about a hundred kilometres from here. Now, I rely entirely on the tribals. They bring me everything I need from that distant village."

Dr. Rishi took a deep breath and continued, "There was someone I knew, my colleague. She would've been willing to die for me, for my research, if I had asked. But I couldn't bear to drag her into a miserable life in the jungle. I knew that if I got success, she would be the happiest person on earth. It was only a matter of a few years. Maybe... maybe my flaw was that I loved science more than anything else."

Manish could see the pain etched on his face as he spoke. This was someone he loved, yes, but perhaps even more than that, someone he deeply respected. Manish felt happy as his thoughts matched.

After lunch, the two of them returned to the laboratory. Manish noticed the drawer labelled "Product" was half open. Inside the drawer was a ring. By now, he had so much faith in Dr. Rishi that he wasn't even surprised. He picked it up and saw, it was a replica of his ring. Even the scratches and dents were identical.

Manish asked him, "How could this invention be useful to mankind?"

Dr. Rishi looked visibly annoyed. As he paced the room, he said, "It's not the scientist's job to decide whether something will help mankind or not. Einstein, Niels Bohr paved the way to unlock the hidden power inside atoms. That discovery is being used to kill people. But it's also the main energy source for our present and future. If dynamite and explosives hadn't been invented, would civilisation, especially in hilly regions, have developed so much? Not at all. Yet those are also the deadliest weapons known to man. You don't need to think on such a grand scale. What about fire? It was science's first discovery. Fire pushed civilisation forward, but its misuse can convert everything to ashes. Or take water, another name for life. But doesn't water also cause death?"

After speaking nonstop for a while, Dr. Rishi calmed down. Leaning back in his chair, he continued, "If you're talking about usefulness, then the potential is enormous. The entire production system of the future could change. We wouldn't need thousands of factories to make different things. At the root of everything are those same 118 elements. If you could load those elements into a machine and operate it correctly, anything could be copied."

Without thinking, Manish blurted out, "Even humans?"

Dr. Rishi didn't respond. He seemed lost in deep thought.

Manish repeated, "Even humans?"

Dr. Rishi looked at him. Manish had never seen such a deep gaze before. Slowly, he replied, "Yes, even humans. That means life itself. The fifth dimension! That's the next phase of my invention. From three to four, then five. Theoretically, I'm confident it's possible. But,"

"But, what?"

"But the experiment hasn't been done yet. If you're willing, you could help me. I promise you won't be harmed."

Manish was a bit startled by Dr. Rishi's words. Still, he said, "Explain to me exactly what you want to do. Then I might agree."

Dr. Rishi said, "Just like we copied your ring, we can copy you. That part poses no issue. First, we'll need to scan your entire body. Then we'll place the elements in the correct positions and trigger a biochemical reaction. But the real challenge is the next step, instilling life. No one in the world can definitively say what life is. But from what is known, and based on my own research, I'm convinced it's possible. The next phase would involve storing all your feelings. Then, using shock therapy, those feelings would be transmitted to the duplicate's brain and vital parts. The fifth dimension, in my view. I've already built the machine for that. But since I haven't found a volunteer, I haven't been able to carry out the experiment."

"You'll release me after the scan. The complexity begins only in the later stages. So, I don't see any danger. I'm in. But the issue is something else. The idea of my duplicate is thrilling. It wouldn't be like a twin brother, it would be me, exactly me. So, I'm wondering what place that copy would have in this society."

Dr. Rishi leapt up from his chair and shouted, "Ah! That same question again! If you want to pursue science, then do it. If not, don't. You can't practice science by worrying about 'what will happen if...'"

He sank back into the chair. With his head buried between his hands on the table, he was breathing heavily. After about a minute of silence, Dr. Rishi's voice returned. He sounded utterly broken.

"I know I'll never get to carry out this experiment. If I wanted, I could've misled those tribal people, tempted them with money, and done it long ago. But I've never learned deceit, and I never will." He paused, exhaled deeply, and added, "Forgive me, young man. I shouldn't have gotten so emotional. Forgive me. Forgive me."

Manish said, "Doctor, I'm ready."

Dr. Rishi slowly lifted his head. His grief-stricken face gradually lit up with joy. Two teardrops shimmered at the corners of his eyes. He stood up, leaned close to Manish's face, and whispered, "Sure? Are you sure?"

"Yes. I have decided."

"Then there's no time to waste. I promised to send you back tomorrow. So, let's start right now. Your mental and physical analysis alone will take several hours. Then we'll have the night for production. Come, come my boy."

However, Sir, I have a condition. I will not go alone. I will take you with me to my village, my home. I feel you shall not disagree, as I agreed to volunteer myself for your research." Manish put the condition. "After visiting my home, you can decide whether you would come back here or not."

Dr Rishi got a little impatient, "When my experiment is over, I shall follow whatever you say. Even if you tell me to die, I surely but a little thought came to my mind, why do you want to take me to your home?"

Manish took a deep breath and said, "That can be discussed later. Now, let us focus on your final experiment of creating a human, with its soul." Dr Rishi agreed as he was super excited to complete his dream.

Recreating Life:

Dr. Rishi walked to a corner of the Machine and pressed a switch. A chair slid out from the wall. He gestured for Manish to sit on it and said, "First, let's begin with your mental analysis. I'll describe to you a few situations, some joyful, some sorrowful, some that invoke respect, and others that may provoke disgust. Based on these, you'll recall memories from your past. My machine will record your brain waves and nerve activity under each emotional condition."

As he spoke, he attached various sensors to Manish's head, chest, and hands. The moment he switched on a few buttons, several large tape spools began to rotate simultaneously.

Then he asked, "Are you ready?"

"Yes, ready," Manish replied.

"Good. Now think about your father, your mother, your loved ones. Your uncle, your elder cousins, think, think. Think of all those you respect."

After a moment of silence, Dr. Rishi continued, "Now think of your deepest sorrows. The major griefs in your life. Think of those moments."

A little later, he added, "Now think of your happiest memories. When you passed your exams. When you got your first job. Think about your sister, as you said that you love her most. You must recall those joyful times."

This process went on for thirty to forty minutes. Then Dr. Rishi switched off the machine. He removed the sensors and asked Manish to get up from the chair. He opened the drawer marked "Source" on the left. That's when Manish noticed how large the drawer really was, big enough to fit one person.

On Dr. Rishi's signal, Manish climbed in and lay down inside it. He strapped him in with a few belts so he wouldn't move. He handed Manish a button-like device and said, "If you feel scared or uncomfortable, just press this. I'll pull you out immediately." Dr. Rishi assured him there was nothing to fear. The scan would be done within an hour, and then he would be brought back out.

The drawer closed. As promised, about an hour later, Dr. Rishi opened it, and Manish came out. To be honest, the doctor's confidence had been so convincing that Manish hadn't felt scared at all. But the thought still haunted him: What if a duplicate is truly created? Then what? Not that he had the courage to express it aloud.

It was evening. Dr. Rishi said, "Let's go for a short walk and get some fresh air. Once dusk falls, we can start the production process. Tonight, as you sleep, you will be... reborn." His voice trembled slightly as he said that. Something inside Manish's chest also stirred.

Around seven o'clock in the evening, Dr. Rishi started the machine. They turned off all the lights in the laboratory and stepped outside. Dr. Rishi carefully locked the iron door from the outside. Neither of them said a word. Though standing beside each other, they felt worlds apart.

Like a machine, Dr. Rishi mechanically prepared dinner, the same menu as lunch. They ate silently and lay down. Neither of them seemed to fall asleep, likely due to the excitement.

At the crack of dawn, Dr. Rishi finished his bath and started preparing breakfast. Manish washed his face in the meantime. As they sat at the breakfast table, Dr. Rishi said, "Remember today's date. The greatest invention in human history is about to be proven today. Everything is complete now. All that remains is to open the door to meet your duplicate. Not just in appearance. But in sorrow, joy, anger, grief, every emotion, everything is perfectly like you. Of course, only if the expressions were correctly captured during yesterday's mental analysis."

Manish asked, "And what if they weren't?"

Dr. Rishi flinched. A piece of bread slipped from his hand onto the floor. "What do you mean? What are you trying to say?"

Manish replied, "I should tell you the truth. No matter how hard I tried, my stream of thought wasn't flowing correctly. At first, it was fine. But when you asked me to think about my uncle… everything went haywire. I have terrible rage toward him. He deceived my father and took everything from us. That betrayal led to my father's cerebral haemorrhage. I had to quit my studies and join the Air Force. Even when you asked me to think of happiness and success, all I could see was his face. I felt like choking him if he had been in front of me.

And when you mentioned my sister, even that filled me with sorrow instead of joy. Because yesterday was the day her Ph.D viva. I wasn't there to hear from her. She must be crying in disappointment."

Dr. Rishi suddenly pushed the table in front of him and bolted out of the room. The cups and plates on the table crashed loudly onto the floor. Manish ran after him. The doctor was running toward the laboratory, shouting like a madman. Manish could hear fragments of his cries: "This is a disaster! My invention will give birth to uncontrollable rage, hatred, and despair! A disaster..."

He flung the lab door open with one pull. A burst of warm air, smoke, and a sharp chemical odour rushed out. It was too dark to see clearly, but from what Manish could make out, the entire room had been scorched by fire. Pages of the thick notebook on the table had been shredded into bits. The floor was littered with acid, chemicals, shards of glass, and paper. Every single machine was smashed. The main apparatus at the back had been struck hard with something heavy. It was burned and charred.

Across the table, someone was lying face down, his body burned by flames. Its height and shape were exactly like Manish's. Suddenly, a burst of fire lit up in the centre of the room.

Dr. Rishi and Manish rushed back to a safe distance. The doctor said, "Since the door was shut, the fire lost oxygen and was extinguished, but maybe something had still been smouldering inside."

Manish shouted, "Let's try to put the fire out somehow!"

But Dr. Rishi looked strangely calm. "There's no way to save it now. That room, especially the machinery, holds too many chemicals and flammable materials. The fire will only grow. Let's move further away."

Before their eyes, the entire house burned like a cursed chamber from mythology. The roof and side walls collapsed. After nearly an hour, all that remained was a pile of motionless rubble.

Manish looked at Dr. Rishi. There was a smile on the doctor's lips. Manish thought, Maybe the shock has driven him mad. But soon he understood it wasn't.

He asked, "How can you be smiling after such a massive disaster? Don't you feel even a shred of sorrow?"

Dr. Rishi replied, "What's the use of grieving? I made an attempt. Not every scientific endeavour succeeds. We must accept both success and failure equally. Be practical."

Then, almost to himself, he muttered, "Just one small mistake… and everything was ruined."

Burning with guilt, Manish said, "The fault was mine. If only I had…"

"No, no. You're not to blame," Dr. Rishi interrupted. "You didn't do anything intentionally. It was my mistake; I rushed things too much. I should've explained everything to you more thoroughly. And the biggest mistake was leaving my notebook in the lab that night. If I hadn't, someone might have been able to try again."

"But why are you calling it a failure?" Manish asked. "You succeeded. But…"

Dr. Rishi cut him off. "If and but', these words hold no value in this world. People want to see the result. Anyway, I dared to challenge the Almighty. In the end, I had to retreat. That's the final word. Maybe the Almighty simply doesn't want this to happen."

Dr. Rishi placed a gentle hand on Manish's head and said, "I just want to give you a message. Think big in life, but think deep as well. And always be positive. And one more thing: if someday you find the right platform, you may share my discovery with the world. Most people will dismiss it as a fantasy. But won't there be a few mad ones like me? People who refuse to stop at three? People who push civilisation forward, step four, step five, and beyond?"

The local tribal people came on time. Then it was time to go home. But just before leaving, Manish asked, "Sir, remember your commitment, you have to go with me."

Dr Rishi thought for a moment and said, "But what will I do going there?"

Manish said, "Commitment is commitment, sir. I am not asking you to die, just come to my village with me. Rest, you can find the reason there."

Dr Rishi had to agree, and both closed the door of his house, took essential things they may need to walk in the jungle and left."

Recoronation:

The tribal companions guided Manish and Dr. Rishi through the forest, walking all night until they reached a small town. The first thing Manish did was call his elder sister from a telephone booth. Hearing Manish's voice, his sister and the rest of the family were overwhelmed with joy.

From the tearful tone in his sister's voice, Manish could feel just how deeply worried they had been. Perhaps they had spent the past two days without proper food or rest, frozen in fear, because the news of the plane crash had surely reached Manish's office and, through them, the family.

Manish told his sister not to share the news with anyone else for now, except their neighbour, who could be equally worried. He would call the office himself and inform them, also requesting that the news not be made public. He would rejoin work in a few days, and then everything would be explained. Manish said to her sister, "Just like sunlight bursts through dark storm clouds after heavy rain, something similar seems to be happening in their lives too."

She asked, "What is it? Just come back quickly. Nothing is more important than the fact that you're returning alive."

Manish replied, "You'll see it for yourself very soon."

As soon as Manish and Dr. Rishi reached home, Manish's mother held him tightly in her arms. His father and younger sister became busy welcoming the unknown guest. Only one person stood silently, like a stone statue, her face pale and speechless. Because in just one glance, Manish's elder sister, Dr. Megha, had recognised Dr. Rishi.

Rishi gazed at Megha without blinking. Like a sudden flashback, hundreds of memories began to surface from the shadows of his mind. All his publicly preached philosophies across the world about staying mentally strong, maintaining control over emotions, and keeping feelings within oneself were now flying away like fallen leaves in a storm. Such a great philosopher, such a renowned scientist, yet his eyes were filled with tears.

Rishi stepped forward, took Megha's hands in his own, and in a trembling voice said,

"Sorry, Megha. I was so lost in my invention that I committed a great injustice to you. Please forgive me."

Megha's tears had already rolled down her cheeks and touched her trembling lips. A faint smile of fulfilment flickered on her face. It didn't take long for her to realise that God truly exists. Her seven years of worship and penance had not gone in vain; God had finally looked down upon her.

Rishi had returned to her life.

---END---

Dear Reader,

Thank you for purchasing this book. I sincerely hope you enjoyed reading these stories and found within them some meaningful insights for living a life of dignity and honour.

If you intend to use any part of this book or its stories, **kindly reach out to me first, as this work is protected under copyright registration.**

As I neither have the resources nor the inclination to run an expensive marketing campaign, **may I humbly request you to share this book information/Amazon link/ Pugmark Books website link with your close ones, your WhatsApp groups, or on social media,** only if you genuinely liked the book as a whole or part of it? Your support will encourage me to continue writing and publishing more of my own work. It will also help nurture good reading habits among the younger generation and perhaps rekindle the reading spirit in many seniors.

Wishing you and your loved ones a joyful and fulfilling life ahead

With warm regards,

Subrata Halder

subratahalder.author@gmail.com

9999715748

New Delhi, India.

About the Author

The author is an accomplished writer who has received several prestigious awards for his short stories. An electronics engineer by profession, he spent several decades working with U.S. multinational companies in senior leadership roles. His professional journey allowed him to travel extensively across numerous countries and five continents, enriching his worldview and creative sensibilities. Deeply passionate about writing, he also expresses himself through art and painting. His stories have been adapted for stage plays by prominent theatre groups and have been booked for movies. He currently lives in Delhi, India.

His earlier publications are:

1. **Think Deep Before You Think Big** – (ISBN 978-93-5628-143-1) – First publication. This book is on sales and marketing, especially for individuals who have transitioned their careers from corporate settings to sales and marketing. (Published in June 2022)

2. **Odd Thoughts** – A collection of several articles written in a casual mood. Some are the outcome of innovative thinking, and some are hilarious. Not a very serious effort, but rather a part of learning self-publishing. (eBook in India/ abroad, and Paperback outside India).

3. **The Monk, His Ferrari, and the Fifth Dimension** – (ISBN 978-93-7542-298-3) – A collection of 12 stories. This one is his first sincere effort, after initial learning of the publication process. (Published in January 2026)

4. **Science – Laugh and Learn** – (ISBN: 978-93-5717-528-9) – a popular science book on modern-day innovation we see around us, we use every day, but the majority of people do not know in depth. Good for children to develop their innovative ideas and inclination towards science. They would not realise they are reading a science book, but a story book which hilariously describes scientific phenomena.
(Published in Feb, 2026, Amazon KDP, eBook and Paperback).

5. **The Monk's Path to Joy: The Art of Living Without Leaving Comfort** - Spiritual, love, science. (This book).

Upcoming Books:

English Books

6. **Sales & Marketing Made Easy and Beyond** – Almost everything related to Sales, Marketing, Corporate culture, communication skills, AI, Creativity and innovative mind development. ((**To be published in April, 2026**).

7. **Tales for Young Minds** – a storybook for children

8. **Tales: Reflections of Society** – Storybook for all ages.

বাংলা বই

৯ – **দৃষ্টি** – সুব্রত হালদাররে গল্প সংকলন

১০ – **কাছরে বন্ধু** – ছ◌োটদরে গল্প সংকলন

১১ – **মার্কটেংি আর ইন◌োভশেন** – ওপররে ৫ নম্বর বইটরি বাংলা সংস্করণ।

১২ – **বজি্ঞান – স◌োজাসাপটা** – সহজ সরল ভাষায় আমাদরে দনৈন্দনি জীবনে ব্যবহার্য্য বজি্ঞান এর গভীর আল◌োচনা। যা জানা থাকাটা শুধু প্রয়◌োজনীয় তা না বশে মজার ও বটে। বশিষেত ছ◌োটদরে বজি্ঞানমনস্ক মন গড়ে তুলতে। ওপররে ৪ নম্বর বইটরি বাংলা সংস্করণ।

The title of each book will be finalised prior to publication and may differ from the one mentioned above. You can find them on Amazon by periodically searching using the author's name, Subrata Halder.

You can also buy these books from 'Pugmark Books' website (https://salesskills.co.in/pugmark-books).

I can also assist aspiring writers in publishing their books at a minimal cost to support their dreams, provided the content is reasonably good.

PUGMARK BOOKS

SCIENCE : ART : TRUST : JOY

Pugmark Books Team
NEW DELHI
https://salesskills.co.in/pugmark-books

Note:

www.ingramcontent.com/pod-product-compliance
Lightning Source LLC
Chambersburg PA
CBHW050017170726
48282CB00025B/438
9789357595964